MYTH-BEHAVING

BOOK TWO OF SHIFTERS ANONYMOUS

MJ MARSTENS

Cover: Kadee Brianna at Everly Yours Cover Designs
Formatting: A.J. Macey at Inked Imagination Author Services

CONTENTS

BLURB

It's a bird.

It's a plane.

It's. . . Belle Harper trying to flap away from all her problem.

I thought being a sex addict was bad—but a war with men who can turn into bloodthirsty predators and want to breed me totally tops that. Add on I'm turning into some unknown monster, and I miss the good ol' days where I knew what I was—a dirty little pervert. Luckily, my days as a sex fiend have taught me a trick or two. Dean Stiffdick and Dr. F*ckface might be Tertiaries, but I am woman.

Prepare to hear me roar.

(And after we've won, prepare to hear me moan because nothing gets me hornier than victory.)

WARNING

Myth-Behaving is book two in *Shifters Anonymous*. This reverse harem novel contains language and content for readers 18+.

DEDICATION

For anyone who has ever felt not good enough—STOP.

YOU. ARE. WORTHY.

Please, remember this when you look in the mirror.
Also, for anyone who's wanted to try something crazy—
sexually—Belle encourages trying new things.
Unless it involves porcupines and pizza cutters.
That sounds dangerous.
And kind of intriguing.
Shit. . . anyone else envisioning a dashing naked porcupine
with a strap-on serving piping hot pizza?
No?
Me, neither.
And since you're still reading, this is for Annie and Allison
—my personal AA (Alpha's Anonymous). Thanks for
helping me curb some of Belle's crazier tendencies (i.e.
mine) and keeping me in line—we'll save those for Baba
Yaga.

Chapter 1

Belle

Sweet saints of broken condoms—I'm a werewolf.

There can be no other explanation as I watch coarse hair begin to ripple underneath my skin and poke out of it. Thank those same skanky saints that I'm wearing *nickel* earrings instead of ones made of silver. It's lucky I'm a cheap ass gal with a penchant for clunky, bargain jewelry. I watch in fascinated horror as the fur protrudes from the top of my arm all the way down to my wrist, retracts, and then pushes out again.

It's my own personal train wreck I can't stop staring at.

Something is trying to crawl out of my body. I catch my reflection in the mirror, my eyes wide in abject terror. Too quickly to discern what it is, my face morphs before shifting back to my normal human one. I scream as all my other worries, including my desperate need for a shower, disappear. There's only me in this horrible moment—the moment of truth when I'm about to learn what Dr. Fuckface really did to me.

I take that back.

The door bursts open with Jack and Jude trying to cram into a one-person bathroom—that one person's already in.

My moment of horror is now to be shared with others.

"Get out!" I garble in a strained voice. "This is a personal moment. I'm having an emotional and physical breakdown. Something's happening to me. I'm a werewolf. Drinking blood is *so* not cool."

"That's a vampire, love," Jude corrects gently. "Why don't you come out here? We can see what's wrong."

"I'm changing," I sob. "Changing into some unknown animal. They injected me with something, and now, I think I'm one of you."

I moan this as I walk back into the cabin, and all six of my new friends stare at me with the same horror I just stared at myself with.

"What did they inject you with?!" Sian asks in a whisper.

"I don't know. It was a mistake."

"A mistake?!" Elise snaps. "What do you mean a *mistake*?"

"They were supposed to inject me with something else to make me horny."

Behind me, Jack snorts.

"Why would they need to do that?"

I cut him a quick glare, but answer, "That's what I said! *So* not the point, though. They wanted to make me go into heat, but Doctor Fucktard gave me the wrong shot. Apparently, the dean isn't too worried because now I'm his *guinea pig*. I'm turning into something, and I don't know what."

"That's not good." Arthur mutters.

"That's *definitely* not good," Theo echoes, "because if they're turning her into something, chances are. . ."

He trails off.

"It's a Tertiary," Jude finishes for him.

"Oh, ok—so, I'm going to be big and bad? That's good because I'm on *your* side," I add hastily.

Even though I don't want to be any kind of animal except a human *one.*

"We have to be careful—you don't know about our species in the sense that we've been raised since infancy to be who we are. When we're in our animal form, we share a human brain, but our animals can take over very quickly. If you're a tertiary who's never been subjected to this duality or being a predator around humans, you could maul us," Jude explains.

I stare at him in shock.

"You mean I could eat you...maybe?"

Jack shrugs.

"Maybe."

"But I would never eat you! I swear—well, except out," I clarify, indicating to Sian and Elise. Sian blows me a kiss.

"We know, love. We're not worried about it. We just have some concerns for your safety and ours," she says gently.

"Well, is there a big cage I can get into and shift? How do I even do it?"

"Don't worry," Jack reassures. "We'll walk you through it. It's something naturally that your body does.

"I mean, do I have any control over it?"

"Eventually, you will, but initially, I don't think so—whatever's inside of you wants out," Arthur murmurs.

I make a face.

"Yeah, I know—it's a werewolf!"

Elise chuckles.

"You're not a werewolf. They're not real, but you could be a wolf."

"I have an idea," Jude mutters thoughtfully.

He walks into the bathroom and shuts the door. Seconds

3

later, he crawls out under the jam as his cockchafer flies around me. I hold very still because—while I don't want to hurt his feelings—he's like a little junebug, and I don't want him getting stuck in my hair. After a few trips around me, he slips back under the door jamb, gets dressed, and comes back out. Honestly, I don't see why he just didn't get naked in front of me—it's not like I was going to jump him or anything.

Really...well, probably.

I mean, now would be a perfect time for distraction, right?

"Well, what's your excuse for not taking your clothes off in front of me?" I demand.

Jude just grins.

"I was smelling you."

"I've got something better you could do with me instead of *sniff me*," I mutter under my breath. No one comments on my not-so-subtle sex comments.

"Well," Arthur demands, "what did you smell?"

"Definitely, *something*—but it's not like anything I've ever smelled before. I don't know *what* she is."

"I just want to be a sex addict!" I sob theatrically.

"Listen, we need to get off this ship," Theos interjects. "Chances are the Jackal has gone back to report. They can look up the dock information and figure out where the ship's going. If we go upstream, they won't be expecting us to fight the current. It'll be a race, but we might be able to get somewhere safer, and then, we can address Belle."

Now, normally, the idea of swimming *up* a dirty river in Britain sounds like an awful idea, but considering how I'm covered in piss water and vomit, beggars can't be choosers, right? It's probably the closest thing I'm going to get to a shower and maybe swimming will distract me from what's happening.

4

And what if I'm a badass water Tertiary?!

I'm a dolphin that can jump through hoops of fire and I have a horn...

Wait!

I'm a narwhal—a majestic one!

Yes, I will spear those bastards who did this to me, and then, fuck people with it. It's official. I'm content with being a narwhal and nod in contentment.

"What is she nodding at?" Arthur whispers to Jude.

"I don't know. Love, what are you nodding about?"

"Don't worry—I've come to accept who I am."

Jack just grins, used to my brand of crazy.

"All right then, let's jump overboard. Everyone can swim, right?"

"Yeah, I can swim, but why wouldn't the rest of you just shift," I point to the girls to add, "and fly away?"

"Because they'll be expecting that. If we all stay in our human forms and swim away, we have a better chance of escaping. It might throw off our scents a bit more."

"Gotcha. Ok, let's do this."

I make for the door, but stop when it feels like my bones are snapping inside of me. I look back at the others, a scream caught in my throat.

"Fuck, she's shifting!" Jack says before I feel my body completely contort and twist into something I don't even know.

It happens within seconds, and when my vision refocuses and I stare out, it's at an unfamiliar view. The others are still before me, but I'm much smaller and lower to the ground. My sight is much keener. I feel powerful, sleek —*undefeatable*. My brain is still my own, but I definitely can feel whatever animal's that I am lurking there.

Aggressive.

5

Angry.

Caged.

I look at the others and see their faces of shocked alarm.

And I know...

I'm a monster.

Chapter 2
Belle

on't panic; don't panic.

     I chant this in my head as I look down at my hand—which is not a hand, but a paw.

A massive paw.

Oh—I know *that* paw. Dear God, I'm a lioness! I've been turned into Nala, and Dean Hardwick, a.k.a. Scar, is going to regret the day he killed Mufasa, a.k.a...

Wow.

I'm *really* not making any sense, but I'm going to blame it on my animal brain. Said animal brain rolls its eyes at me. Quite frankly, I don't enjoy its tone, but I'll take it if it means my lion isn't going to eat my friends. Now that I think about it, I don't have *any* urge to eat them. That's great! I start to talk, but it comes out in an odd chuff, and everyone immediately scrambles back.

How to reassure them that I'm not going to eat them?

Looking at my sharp claws, I get an idea. I scratch out 'Not going to eat you' into the hardwood. Good thing we don't have a ticket because someone would definitely sue for repairs—and for bringing animals aboard. I see Jude read my message. Well, I hope he can because a *lioness* wrote it. The gang is still just staring at me with the same shock. Huh...*maybe they weren't expecting me to be this badass?*

Maybe I'm so fucking cool—

Something catches my eye from the corner of my periphery; I turn and give the loudest scream ever—except, do you know how a lion screams? The sound is shrill, hoarse, and absolutely terrifying. It one hundred percent resonates with how I'm feeling because coming out of my ass is my tail—and it's a freaking snake!

You thought that sounded bad?

It gets worse—because coming out of my lower back is a damned goat's head!

"What fresh hell is this?" my lion roars, the goat bleats, and the snake hisses.

I'm not a fucking lioness—I'm...*I don't know what this is!* I'm three animals in one. I try to run away, but the goat and the snake follow because, well, they're attached to me. I run in a circle as my goat screams and my snake tries to bite me, until finally, I roll over—onto the goat, twisting its head in a gruesome manner. The pain, because the damn thing is attached to me, fills my body. Suddenly, I can feel the snapping and twisting of my bones as I shift back into my human form. I lay there naked, panting, traumatized, wondering how much therapy this is going to cost me in the

future.

"For the love of whores, what was that?!" I manage to gasp.

The other six are still standing there frozen.

"What was that?!" I demand again, only louder.

Arthur, my sweet bookworm, steps forward.

"That was...a chimera."

"A who now? A what now? A chi-what?"

"A chimera," he repeats. "It's an animal with the head of a lion, the tail of a snake, and a goat head on the back. It's an animal from Greek mythology."

"No, no, no," I refute, throwing up a hand. "That's not possible because I wanted to be a unicorn, and Dean Prick told me I couldn't because unicorns aren't real. So, how can I be a Greek *mythological* animal if I couldn't be a *unicorn*?"

I mean, what kind of fresh hell is this?!

That asshat—I mean *arse*hat—makes fun of me for wanting to be a unicorn or even a dinosaur because they're extinct, but then he turns me into this crap?! *Oh, man.* Dean Stiffdick is going to get it, and I want it to go on the record that I think this is *all* horseshit. "Dean Hardwick told me that I couldn't be a mythological creature," I pout.

"Yes, I see where he's coming from," Arthur says, "but

this is different—a lion, goat, and snake are living animals. This is more like—"

"Cloning and graphing," Jude finishes for him. "The dean and his scientist are splicing together animal cells to create something new."

"Oh, God—then it's worse than I imagined! I'm their guinea pig for monsters. Oh, why couldn't they have combined me into something way cooler? I'm terrified of snakes!"

"And yours is a real doozy," Arthur comments.

"What's   that mean?!"

"It's a black mamba—it's considered the deadliest snake in the world."

"Oh my God—I can't feel my tail! It's not attached to me even though it's attached to me. What happens if it bites me or somebody else?! Is there any antivenom? We need to go get

antivenom!"

"It did look a little out of hand," Sian notes.

"Thanks," I deadpan. "Maybe we can just cut it off?"

The rest of them look at me like I just said the craziest thing.

"What? Is that like cutting off my arm in human form?"

"Do you know why you shifted back to a human?" Jack says.

"Well, I rolled on my back and twisted the goat's head. Goatee didn't like that much—it hurt *everywhere*!" I respond, remembering the excruciating pain.

Jack nods.

"Yeah, the pain is what shifted you back to being human. Can you imagine what cutting off your snake tail would be like?"

"Oh!" I gasp. "The pain would be...I can't even. But on the bright side, I might never shift again! I'd turn back to a human and probably be so traumatized. Huh, well, things to think about. At least I've got options—terrifying options. Well, listen, I don't feel any urge to shift. Let's get off this boat. Where are my clothes?"

"Erm. . ." Elise mumbles, pointing to a bunch of scraps. "You shifted out of them—that's why we take *off* our clothes."

God damn it, I have to swim in the freaking river naked. Well, fuck it. I've streaked through enough campuses that this shouldn't bother me. I stand up, and everyone gets an eyeful of my goods. I smirk at them.

"Don't act like you're not impressed."

The others look away but Jack sends me a wink—he gets me.

"Here," Jude directs, walking over to the dresser in the cabin and pilfering whoever's clothes. "Put this on," he directs me. "Grab extras," he orders Theo. "Let's get the hell out of here."

This last bit is said to us all. Jude wrenches open the door and marches out. Jack follows, then Arthur. Sian and Elise each take one of my elbows, and Theo takes the rear. We walk over to the side of the boat, and I realize we're quite a ways up. It's not really a boat as much as it's a mother-fucking ship—*and they want me to jump off of it.*

"Are you insane?!" I shriek, but Jude is already swan-diving over the edge.

Yep, he's insane.

And I guess I'm joining the loony bin because Sian and Elise drag me to the ledge, and we all jump in together.

I'm not going to need therapy after this—*I'm going to need a straight jacket.*

Chapter 3

Jude
THE COCKCHAFER

I slam into the cold water of the River Severn, hoping it will clear my head to give me an idea of what to do next—but also to erase the image of Belle *naked*. Unfortunately, I think that image is seared into my brain permanently. The woman is much too perfect for her own good. Thankfully, my mind has something else to focus on other than Belle in the buff—it's her as a chimera. Whenever an image of her jubilees pops up, another of a goat coming out of her arse replaces it. *Effective, albeit disturbing.*

Speaking of disturbing, I love how seven people just jumped off a ship and no one batted an eye. They're not even looking. I peer behind me to make sure everyone is there. I don't know these waters, even though it doesn't seem deep—if a ship can go through it, an even stronger rip current can be lurking beneath. Even the strongest swimmer can drown. I keep glancing behind me periodically, and eventually, I see Belle on her back floating.

"What are you doing?" I yell.

"I'm done swimming—let's just let the current take us!"

"The current's going in the other direction, love. You *have* to swim upstream."

"That's horseshit!" she shouts back.

"No—it's fish—we're in *fish* shit," Jack corrects.

I roll my eyes at his terrible pun.

"Come on, Belle, not much further. We need to make sure that we're heading in another direction to throw off our scent."

We spend the next forty-five minutes trying to uplift one another to go just a little bit further. The only one who doesn't really seem fazed is Theo, who's an avid swimmer in both forms. The bloke was simply born into this lifestyle. God knows how far we go before I finally lead us to the shore. Everyone collapses on the rocky beach, exhausted. Even Theo looks a little worn out.

"Right, what next?" Belle pants. "Can we go stay in a hotel somewhere and sleep? You know, just like pause this whole 'I'm going to get you and kill you or use you as a mass weapon' thing that's going on?"

Jack rolls over with a brow raised.

"I don't think that's how it works."

"*Definitely* not how it works," Arthurs concurs.

"Well, we need to get out of Gloucestershire," Elise annunciates crisply. "Our lives are in danger—Belle's life is in danger!"

Belle simply shrugs nonchalantly.

"They should be afraid—*very* afraid. I'm a lioness with a goat coming out of my ass and a venomous snake that will eat you alive."

She continues to mutter about how B.A. she is; thankfully, Arthur cuts her off before she can really get going.

"Why don't we go up north?" he suggests.

"North where?" Theo asks.

"Up to Scotland. My family has land in the highlands. We can hide there. It's remote and hard to get to."

"Then how the holy hell are we going to get there?" Belle demands.

Arthur leans over and pats her arm.

"Don't worry. My family's lived there for generations, and we'll be safer there. My clan is there and will protect us."

"A clan of horny toads?" Belle wonders.

"Yep, a clan of horny toads."

"Oh, it sounds like my dream home!" she laughs.

"How are we going to get there, though?" Sian wonders.

"The quickest way would obviously be to fly or shift," Theo points out.

"But, but...I don't want to shift!" Belle interjects.

"We know, love, don't worry. How about I call someone who can help us?"

Belle sits up and looks at Jack.

"It's official. You're that guy in the group—the one that has *all* the connections. All right, who you goin' to call?" No one can answer because she yells "Ghostbusters! Get it? Except, they can't help I don't think. We need something like Shifter-Assholebusters!"

Belle hums the movie's theme song while shimming about, and my brain scrambles to not focus on her form clearly outlined through her wet clothes. Instead, I actually ponder who Jack is texting. While I'm eternally grateful to Jep the hound dog for helping us find Belle, I'm leery of who Jack intends to call—not all his connections are...savory. The resourceful man pulls out his phone, which is dripping wet, and shakes it off before proceeding to text the mystery person.

"Is that thing even working?" Theo queries.

"Yeah, I have the new iPhone II pro. You can get it wet, and it'll still work."

"Huh," Theo mumbles, "I just stick mine in a polybag."

"K, I got someone coming. They'll be here shortly," Jack announces. "Until then, we can just lay here and get dry."

"Can you take a picture of me with your phone?" Belle asks Jack. "I want to see how indecent this white T-shirt looks on me."

Arthur and Theo groan, making Sian and Elise giggle.

"Very indecent," Sian reassures the wayward Yank.

"Want to trade tops?" Belle jokes, wagging her eyebrows at my freckled friend.

The three birds flirt with one another, and I have to adjust myself. I can tell that the other three guys are just as uncomfortably turned on as well.

"Ladies," Arthur says, clearing his voice, "we should talk about—"

But his sentence is cut off by the sound of something running up on us *quickly*. Without thinking, I command Belle to shift. She looks over at me with startled eyes. It's obvious she doesn't know how to do it yet, anyway. All of us tense as an arse jumps from the brush.

"Hey!" Jack shouts, jumping up and rushing over to the donkey. "He made it!"

The donkey shifts back into his human form and the man stands there unabashedly naked.

"Hello there, ladies," he drawls slowly, winking at them.

"They're lesbians," I announce flatly.

"Oh, hey, Papa Roach!" Harry calls to me, reminding me why I hate his guts so much—no wonder Jack didn't tell me who he was calling. "Ah, they're just lezzies 'cause they haven't had the right dick yet."

The git winks at them again, and I swear Belle might be drooling. I clear my throat loudly to get her attention.

"*This* is who you called?!" I hiss to Jack, who looks a little sheepish

"We needed somebody that we could use to ride!" he defends.

"I'm going to be riding him?" Belle cuts in with far too much interest.

"Oh, you can ride me—" the arse starts.

"Ok, that's it! Belle, you can be on Jack's back, and Arthur and Theo, you both can ride Harry."

My two best mates swivel around to glare at me.

If looks could kill, I'd be one dead papa roach.

Chapter 4
Belle

*B*eing a sex addict, usually you can spot one of your kind right away—and Harry is clearly a fiend of bumping uglies. Jude says that he's Jack's cousin. *So does that make him an ass, too?* I wonder in my head. And then I think, oh, my god, his parents named him *Harry Ass*. I giggle and point this out. Harry puffs up with importance.

"I tell you, Harold is a right proper name—it's the name of kings. And I'm not an ass; I'm actually a pack mule—as in I'm *packing*."

"Ok, we get it!" Jude snaps.

He really doesn't seem to like Harry very much.

"The quickest way to get to my family," Arthur cuts in, easing the tension, "is for us to shift. Belle, we know that's not going to be possible for you right now; so, you're going to need to ride. Theo obviously can't shift either, and it's hard for me to keep up. Jude, Elise, and Sian will fly. You'll ride Jack, and Theo and I will ride Harry."

Arthur says this flatly and doesn't look very pleased—

nor does Theo—but, apparently, me riding Jack is better than me riding *Harry*.

"Now that we've gotten that I'm Harry—and I'm hung—who are you?" the pack mule cousin asks as he saunters over, his junk twitching.

I try to keep my eyes on his without looking south.

"I'm Belle. Nice to meet you," I answer, holding out my hand and showing that I can be a proper American person with polite manners.

"Belle, what a delicious name. And what kind of shifter are you?"

"I'm a chimera," I announce.

"Oh, chimera..." Harry starts before pausing. "A what's it?"

"Yeah, that's what *I* said but Arthur informed me..." I pause, wondering if maybe I shouldn't be telling this to a stranger, even if he is Jack's cousin.

"You can tell him, love," Jack reassures me. "He's good for it, even if he is a little stupid."

Harry snorts.

"He's just jealous. I'm hung as well as ridiculously smart and good looking."

This dude seems almost as full of himself as well, I am. But then again, if you've got it, flaunt it—and Harry's got it.

"Ok," I nod, "I trust Jack if he trusts him. I was just human, and then, I was turned into this chimera."

This announcement has Harry's attention.

"*What?!* You were *human* and *turned* into whatever?"

"It's a long story," Jude sighs, "and we've got to get going. Belle can tell you when she's riding Jack, and it'll be great because you can just shut up and listen."

I laugh.

"What's Jude's problem?" I whisper to Sian and Elise.

"He's jealous." Sian says with excitement.

"Of Harry? Why? Oh—because he has such a big penis? I've seen Jude's ham candle—he has nothing to be jealous of!"

Elise chuckles.

"No—Jude's jealous because he thinks that you're into Harry!"

"I'm not!" I swear. "Totally not into Harry—*just his dick*. And can you blame me? Look at the thing!"

Elise slaps my arm lightly.

"You know what I mean—*Jude likes you*."

"Yeah, but why isn't he jealous of the other guys then?"

Sian and Elise shrug.

"We're kind of a family, the six of us, and you're someone special that we've let in. Even though Jack has all these connections, and obviously, we have family, we really don't let a lot of people into our circle."

I smile at her explanation, touched to be included.

"All right. We're going to shift and fly overhead. If you need anything, call out to us," Sian directs.

I nod and thank them before turning around to see that Jack's already turned. Jude helps me onto his back.

"I overheard the birds tell you already, but remember if you need anything, just holler."

I realize he's going to be turning into his bug and flying overhead. I try not to shudder.

"*Don't* fly into my hair," I command sternly, making him smirk.

"Quit telling me what to do, and I might not."

I quickly zip my lips. If he flies into my hair there's a good chance I'll involuntarily smash him, and then, I would be devastated. Harry shifts into his pack mule, and Theo jumps on holding a shifted Arthur in his arms.

"Why isn't Arthur hopping—erm, running?" I wonder.

"It's just easier this way. He's light enough to hold, and he's not meant to travel long distances on foot," Theo fills in.

We start making our way North, and the silence reminds me that I'm supposed to be talking.

"Ok, so my story, huh? Well, I guess I need to tell you guys anyways what happened," I state since I never told everyone what happened with Dr. Fuckface and Dean Firm-Phallus did. This is going to take a while..."

Theo shrugs.

"We're going to the Highlands via donkey; it's going to take a bit. On the bright side, though, Jack and Harry are strong and are able to go for a long time."

Harry makes some muffled sound, and I stifle a laugh. I don't speak ass, but I'm pretty for sure he just said, *That's what she said!*

Pulling myself together, I think of where to begin. It's a pretty convoluted story, but it all comes back to one thing—

"Once upon a time, there was a sex addict..."

Chapter 5

Belle

arry the Pack Mule gives me a side look, as if to say, *"A sex addict?"*

"Yes," I confirm, assuming this is what he's thinking, "and that sex addict was me—*is* me."

The pack mule waggles his eyebrows. It is both disturbing and hilarious because I didn't know donkeys could do that. Jack tries to kick him with his hind legs from the side and almost tips me off.

"Behave," I tut at him before snapping to Harry, "and you focus! I swear you need the help almost as much as I do, you horndog! *This* is how it all started. A wink here, an innuendo there—it's a slippery slope, I tell you! And once you start falling down it, you can't climb back up. *I* knew I needed to get some help; so, I went to Sexaholics Anonymous. Except, well, that turned out to be...Theo, what are you guys?"

"Shifter's Anonymous," he reminds me. "It's a group we started for Primaries who just didn't feel like they had a place in the world."

Arthur croaks sadly.

"Well, I think it's a wonderful group. I know that Jude said you tend to just stick together with your own kind, but I think it's marvelous you've branched out and made friends. I especially love that you all accept one another in a world that Jude said isn't very accepting. But, going back, I didn't know that everyone there at Shifter's Anonymous was a shifter—I didn't even know what a shifter was! I thought they were all normal human sexaholics...if you would call that *normal*. In fact, I'm pretty for sure our first three meetings were just absolute miscommunication—I thought everyone was hitting on me in a really weird British way!" Jack lets out a donkey snort, making me chuckle. "Well, you can't blame a gal for hoping! Anyway, it turns out that they can turn into animals, which now leads us to Dean Stiffdick and Dr. Fuckface."

"Who?" Theo wonders.

"Oh, Dean Hardwick and his...I don't know, scientist doctor? Oh, and don't forget about his henchmen, or animal minions—we'll get to his minions—but yeah, it's mainly the dean and doc I don't like. So, apparently, Dean Hardwick is teaming up with Dr. Fuckface—who turns into what animal, I have no clue; I just assume some sort of Tertiary—anywho, they are using women like me *to breed*."

Theo scratches his head.

"That doesn't make any sense—you're *human*."

At this, one of Harry's ears turns sideways in what I assume must be curiosity.

"I *was* human," I explain. "Well, I think I'm still human. Maybe. No, not really. Nope. Dr. Fuckface threw all my human dreams out the window—human dreams I didn't even know I had! See, I *was* human, and they were just going to use me to breed. Apparently, there's something special about my blood," I clarify to Theo. "I don't know what it is, and I have no idea what they're looking for but I think that maybe there's something about me that makes it so you guys can breed at any time."

Theo scratches his chin thoughtfully.

"Kind of wish you weren't in toad form," he complains to Arthur. "But if I had to hazard a guess, it's about our unique reproductive cycles. As Shifters, we have to follow the rules of our animals to reproduce. So as a slippery dick, my parents have to mate in water and lay eggs."

"Whoa, whoa, whoa!" I tut, holding out a hand. "You came from an egg?!"

"I mean, technically, we all come from eggs," Theo replies.

"You know what I mean! Like, your mom popped out an egg, and then, you popped out later?"

Theo chuckles.

"Yes."

"Well, how did she know where to find you? And did she like, scoop you up and stick you in an aquarium at home for safety?"

"Actually, that's *exactly* what she did. So many of our kind don't make it because of how we're born. That's why my mum basically incubated me at home like a pet fish. Out of hundreds of eggs, I'm the only one that survived," he finishes with a sigh.

I look at him.

"That's terrible."

Theo shrugs pragmatically.

"It's just how our kind is. It's hard because you're born as the animal you are but once you make that first shift back into becoming human, you stay that way until after a certain age. I think this is a defense mechanism that shifters have so that there isn't any go between when you're younger and can't consciously control it. Can you imagine if I were a baby, and I just shifted into a slippery dick in public or shifted into a slippery dick while my mum was on the balcony and she dropped me from the first floor[1]?"

I cringe.

It's a good thing that evolution was thinking about these shifters...can you imagine dropping something from the second *floor?!*

"So, you're fish, and then one day—*boom*—you're a cute, squalling baby?"

"Pretty much. My mum said it happened within hours of birth. My parents got to enjoy the entire process of having a human baby. Shifter reproduction is...tricky. For my mum, all she had to do was lay her eggs, but mammal shifters have to carry their babies in their animal forms. Think about elephant shifters—you have to stay in your animal form for almost two years. That's a lot of time to be gone from the human world, who doesn't know we're shifters. It's why we cloister with our kind—because they understand our needs as the animal we are and are the most supportive of those animalistic demands."

"Wow, that sounds beyond difficult. I can't imagine being pregnant for two years—heck, I can't imagine even being an elephant! But I think it would be fun to have a trunk."

"Really. Why's that?" Theo asks.

"Don't you think it would be fun to suck up water and spray yourself for a DIY shower whenever? Or shove your trunk up somebody's ass?" Theo just blinks at me, and I clear my throat. "Sorry. Go on. I'm listening."

My slippery dick quirks a smile before continuing.

"As I was saying, we stay in human form until we hit puberty. Then, we have our second shift. From that point on, we learn how to shift back and forth and how to control it so we don't do it in public. The first rule any shifter is taught is that humans can't know about us. Our species is a secret. Other than that, the chain of command has been drilled into us since birth—Tertiaries, Secondaries, Primaries. And as Primaries, we are nothing. We will always be the lowest of the lowest, and we must follow the food chain unless we want to die."

Jesus on Wheat Thins—the Tertiaries really add new meaning to *'alpha a-hole'*.

"And if you ever want any kids?" I prompt.

"I have to find another slippery dick—we can only mate within our own species and only when we are in animal form."

"Which is where I come in," I breathe, understanding dawning on me. "There's something special about my blood, even though I'm human. I think that they want to use me as a breeder because—"

"Because it sounds like any shifter can breed with you without any of the restrictions," Theo finishes.

"Well, joke's on them—they meant to make me go into heat to breed me...instead, they injected me with some diabolic concoction Dr. Fuckface made." Again, one of Harry's ears quirks. "That's right—they turned me into *a monster*. Thanks to Dr. Fuckenstein, I'm a pussy on roids with a caprine, serpentine ass—*not* the animal, though."

It's like the Universe doesn't want me to get laid.

Challenge accepted, Bitch.

Chapter 6

Arthur

THE HORNY TOAD

I listen in horror as Theo and Belle come to the same conclusion that I have—the Tershes have found a way to use somebody as a breeder and not just anyone, *but humans*. There must be something special about their blood, as Belle said, that alerts the Tertiary—something they've found that the rest of us haven't even thought to look for. *Then again, why would we?* We're just Primaries. The Tershes are the ones in power, and so they crave more of it.

If they can create a mass army of their kind, why wouldn't they?

The implications are enough to make your stomach drop out your arse.

I have so many questions...

Is Belle the first one that they've found, or do they have other innocent, human women put away?

Have they already been bred?

Is an army already amassing?

Not to mention the shot that doctor...well, I don't really know his real name, Dr. *FuckFace* gave Belle—it's created a monster—*how many others have they already made?*

Are they waiting to take over control of the world to over-power and subdue humans?

My mind whirls while Belle regales Harry with funny tales about her miscommunications with us. I twitch on Harry's back, wondering what can be done—*if anything.* Jude buzzes over my head and chitters. He's much like me, logical, worried, wanting to fix, and solve everything. All we've ever wanted to do is make the world a better place for our kind—to show that Primaries are equals—but what's going on with Belle supersedes everything.

The question is, what can we do about it?

We don't only endanger our own kind, but ourselves, our family, and other loved ones.

What do we have to offer as mere *Primaries?*

Two hours later, we're finally in Nottingham. Belle is making jokes in reference to some daft Yank movie called *Robin Hood, Men In Tights*. I still have no answers, but I'm relieved that we're finally going to be meeting my cousin at the station and I shift back into human form. My cousin will have clothes for everyone. We can change, and then I can finally head home. My Ma and Da will not be delighted about this, but they always have my back.

That's more my Scottish roots than my shifter roots— the clan sticks together *no matter what.*

I feel bad for Sian and Elise. Since they've chosen each other, both their parents have turned them out. It's a slap in the face for our kind to go outside of your species. My parents will feel no differently about the friends I've chosen, but they're Scots before shifters. Our morals come first, and we stand for what's right and help those in need.

We hide behind some small bushes while Theo goes to find my cousin. He comes back with our clothes so we can all change since being starkers is frowned upon at the through station. While we dress, Belle stares at us with the same hungry, unabashed interest that we all look at her with. I think that's the thing I love most about her—her unapologetic honesty about who she is and what she wants. Society has made her feel bad about her choices, but I don't think Belle feels bad about them.

If Oxford were a different place, Belle wouldn't change a single thing. She doesn't have a problem with who she is—she loves herself, and *I* love that about her. It speaks of a bravery that I don't have. When you're Primary, you've been cut down your entire life. Belle, on the other hand, has that voice she isn't afraid to use.

She is a chimera—hear her roar.

I quickly put on my pants and button down, take her hand, and lead her over to my cousin, Dageus, who was waiting to escort us back home. He clasps me in a tight bear hug before stepping back to examine Belle.

"Are you a horny toad?" he demands.

"I'm horny," she admits.

I palm my face and laugh.

"She's something out of this world," I tell Dageus, "and don't worry about it. We'll address it later. Suffice to say we need your help."

"I know. We got your message. Your parents are waiting, as are mine. Don't worry. The clan will help you no matter what."

I smile.

"That's exactly what I'm hoping for."

We all clamber onto the train. Dageus was kind enough

to get us a private compartment, but it's tight with nine people.

"Holy titties, it's hot in here," Belle moans. "Hotter than two mice fucking in a wool sock."

Dageus blinks at her.

"What? You guys don't have that saying here?"

"No," I chuckle. "We don't use sayings about animals... you know, because we're shifters."

"Huh, well, I never thought about that," she hums. "I wonder if mice shifters *do* fuck in wool socks..."

Dageus just looks at her, not sure what to think, and I love it. My cautious, reserved cousin is totally charmed by the vivacious Yank. Dageus must see something on my face because a look of horror washes over his before he points at Belle and blurts out:

"Is this your girlfriend?!"

I glare at him, feeling my cheeks heat and sheepishly look over at Belle.

"I'm sorry—what was I supposed to think?" Dageus continues, oblivious. "You're sitting there, giving her calf-eyes and mooning over her!"

"Would you shut your geggie[1]?!" I snap.

Belle comes to my rescue by looking Dageus right in the eye and saying, "No, I'm not dating Arthur, but I would be honored to be his girlfriend because he is sweet, kind, and so very smart. And it's rare in this world to find somebody who is willing to go the distance that he—and everyone else here—has gone to help me."

Dageus nods.

"Yes, he's a true Scotsman."

Belle laughs.

"Yes, he is. He's the best one that I know."

"How many more do you know, lass?" Dageus wants to know.

"Well...just you. So, no offense, but Arthur is my favorite. Since we're going to Scotland, I suppose I'll be meeting a lot more of you; maybe after that I can make a different assessment," she teases, winking at me.

I know she's joking, but I sincerely hope that she doesn't meet my cousins and find me lacking. They're all taller, stronger—*not as red-headed.* But she seems to read my mind because she rests an arm around me and croons:

"But I probably can meet every person in Scotland, and they'll never measure up to Arthur. I think you're pretty awesome, Dageus, and I appreciate how you're going to be helping me—especially my friends, too—knowing that's not how shifters normally operate. But Arthur—he's a one-of-a-kind horny toad."

She smiles at me, her eyes shining, *and I fall head over heels in love with her all over again.*

Chapter 7
Belle

"So where does your clan of horny toads live?" I wonder. "I hope it's Hogwarts."

Arthur rolls his eyes.

"I hate to disappoint you—but it's not."

"Nope," Dageus agrees. "Our clan has land right by Loch Kemp."

"Never heard of it."

"Oh, it's fairly large, but it stems from Loch Ness itself."

"Now, *that* I've heard of. More accurately, the *Loch Ness Monster.*" I gasp, "Oh, my gosh! Is the Loch Ness Monster real?!"

"Ach, of course, it's real!" Dageus confirms. "Only a fool wouldn't think so."

"Have you seen it?"

"Nay."

"Then, how do you know it's real?"

Arthur answers for his cousin by touching his nose, which twitches.

"We can *smell* it."

"What does the Loch Ness Monster smell like?" I wonder.

"Danger," Jude frowns with a nod. "That's a Tertiary if I've ever met one."

"Wait, the Loch Ness Monster is a shifter?" I cross my arms over my head. "You know, Dean Stiffdick told me that dinosaurs were extinct. So, I don't understand how Nessie can be real."

"Why, the Loch Ness Monster isn't a dinosaur, lass," Dageus responds.

"What the hell is it then?"

"We don't know. It keeps to itself, and we keep to ours."

I crinkle my nose at this.

"I don't know about you guys, but I'd be asking a shit ton more questions right now. Also, I don't think I'd be living so close to this known monster without having answers to said questions. Heck, I don't even think if I had the answers that I'd be living there! Are you sure this place is safe?" I whisper to Jude.

"It's safe," he reassures.

"Only because Loch Kemp is too small for the Loch Ness Monster to get to," Jack adds.

He winks at me.

I don't know if he's joking or not.

"Don't worry about this monster," Arthur reassures. "You're going to love the Highlands."

"Why's that?"

"There's no place on Earth like the Highlands."

"Aye, he's right," Dageus agrees. "No place at all. It's magical—it's the Land of the Fae."

I feel my brows rise.

"I thought that was Ireland? And FYI...no one wants

anything to do with those tricky bastards." Dageus shushes me in mild panic.

"The Fae live all over, and don't be talking about the wee folk like that—they'll hear you!"

"In a fucking train they'll hear me?! Jesus, those Fae bitches have everything rigged."

Arthur clamps a hand over my mouth.

"Are you *trying* to jinx us?"

"No, I'm trying to get the hell out of here without meeting any Fae! Christ, all I wanted was a trolley cart with some fucking chocolate frogs—I mean...oh, man, I'm sorry! Have I insulted you guys? That's just from *Harry Potter*. I swear I don't eat chocolate *real* frogs *or* toads. I have a mild obsession with *Harry Potter*. I still dream of getting an owl letter one day—preferably by one with a huge set of hooters."

Now, there's an image for you.

Jack and Theo are trying to stifle their grins, and Jude just puts a hand to his face like he's used to my shenanigans. Poor Dageus, though, probably doesn't know what to make of me. And Harry...Harry stares at me like I'm his favorite thing in the world—*and he hasn't even seen my tits yet!*

Makes you wonder why the others aren't looking at me the same way since they have.

"Well, fairies aside, I'm sure the Highlands are beautiful," I attempt to remedy my word vomit. "I'm sure it's much better than where I come from."

"Where are you from, lass?" Dageus asks.

"The Midwest—Nebraska. Do you know what there is to see in Nebraska?" Everyone in the cart shakes their head. "Nothing," I fill in for them, "*absolutely nothing.* But I have a good family. It's just my parents and me...I think they had me and realized they didn't really want to chance having more, er, like me."

Everyone in the cart chuckles

"Were you a cheeky, little nipper?" Sian wonders.

"Huh?"

Sian rolls her eyes.

"Were you a bit of a troublemaker?" she clarifies.

"*A bit* is putting it mildly—I was hell on wheels. Luckily, I rerouted all that energy into sexual escapades when I got older."

"Ooo, yes, do tell me more," Harry purrs.

Jack leans over and smacks his cousin upside the head.

"Behave."

"I'm not the one who brought it up!" Harry gripes under his breath, put out.

I chuckle at his pouting face.

"Maybe another time I'll regale you with tales of my sexual exploits."

Harry immediately perks back up.

"Can't wait!" he chirps, and even Dageus—who I can tell really doesn't approve of me—looks mildly intrigued.

But being the stuffy pot he is, he gets back down to business.

"My da's most interested in hearing what you have to say," he tells Arthur before addressing the rest of us. "My da's Laird—that's the name of the clan leader. I told him of your urgent matter, and I'm hoping he'll help us even though it doesn't pertain to horny toads."

I look at him askance.

"What are you talking about?! It most certainly *does* pertain to horny toads! Just because it didn't happen to you, per se, doesn't mean it doesn't affect your species—this

34

affects all Primaries! It affects all shifters! This is huge. This is—"

Jude cuts me off.

"This is life or death right now for us," he simplifies. "We have a war on our front we didn't even know was coming. I think the Tertiaries want to exterminate the humans and use the others as breeders. Even if we don't care about the humans—no offense, Belle—we're still part of the world. If the Tershes can cut them out, who's to say they won't do the same to us?"

Harry shrugs nonchalantly, like none of this bothers him.

"I doubt it," he disagrees. "The Tershes need us to do their bitch work."

Elise puts her arms under her impressive bosom.

"I don't want to be anyone's *bitch*—and certainly not the Tershes! So, yes, it does affect us and I'm not going to take it lying down."

"Would you take it standing up?" Harry asks hopefully.

I laugh because I feel like he's the male version of me— and really, one of me was too much already.

I don't think this group can handle two of us.

Jack leans over to smack his cousin again.

"Seriously, shut your mouth so your arse quits talking from it."

"Where else is my arse supposed to speak from?" Harry demands.

Theo ignores everyone and looks to Arthur.

"How long from Nottingham to White Bridge?"

"Just a couple of hours by train. Then, we'll have to take a small jaunt to Loch Kemp. My uncle will be meeting us, Dageus' dad."

"The Laird?" I clarify.

35

"Yep."

"Awesome, I can't wait to meet him."

Dageus and Arthur look a bit nervous at this.

"Listen, lass," Dageus begins, "my Da is—"

Arthur cuts him off.

"He's how you'd say—"

"*Old school*," Jack finally interjects for them both.

"By the books." Theo adds.

"Follows the rules," Jude continues.

"I get it!" I laugh, throwing up my hands. "I understand what all those things are. We say them in America, too. I need to watch my mouth, keep my legs crossed, and not hit on him, right?"

Harry smirks.

"You can save all that for me, love."

This time it's Jude who lunges for him, and Jack has to pull him back.

"Woah, woah, Papa Roach! Take a joke," Harry tuts, and Jude slumps back down in the train seat, glaring daggers at the man. "You all need to lighten up. If we have a war coming on, this might be the last time anyone get some laughs—or sex—for that matter."

I gasp in distress at this.

No more time for sex?!

That's not war—*that's the world coming to an end.*

36

Chapter 8

Sian
THE TITMOUSE

When I was just an ankle biter, my family took a trip to Loch Ness. My brother and I were obsessed with the fact that there could be a giant monster living in the murky waters. Of course, we didn't find anything, but I learned two things that summer:

One—while the Highlanders were friendly, they did not take to strangers kindly. They tolerated us at best.

And two: You never, ever go outside of your flock.

Another family of shifters was vacationing at the same time we were—the Highlands make a great holiday spot for my kind because it's so remote. Blackbirds aren't exceptionally special in regards to shifters, but they're at the top of the Primary food chain. Their daughter had been around my age, and we got along well playing together—until her parents and my parents found out, that is. That's when I learned the hard lesson that you don't go outside your species. *Even though we were both birds, we were not birds of a feather.*

Unfortunately, where I lived, we didn't have very much extended family. I didn't grow up alone; I had an older brother, but he just did his own activities. I always think about poor Elise, who was an only child. At least I had my brother—she had no one. When I moved to Banbury, I became closer to my cousin in Oxford. She and I are close in age, and my parents approved of that friendship.

But the one I have with Elise?

Not on your Nelly.

Sad thoughts and memories bring me back to the Highlands, where I am once again. I stare at the breathtaking beauty of the expanse of land as we disembark from the train. As Arthur said, his uncle is there waiting for us. His look is the all too familiar one I remember from when I was a little girl and we vacationed here—polite but restrained, certainly *not* welcoming. I feel my muscles tense with the urge to shift and fly away from it all.

Not only is Arthur's uncle the clan leader, but he's also a shifter—*two marks against anyone who is not of his kind.* And here Arthur is bringing seven other people home who are nothing like him. My stomach flutters nervously for my friend. I don't want his parents to do what my parents did—what Elise's parents did—and completely cut Arthur from their lives. Humans need connection with one another; they need that interaction. Shifters need it on a completely different level, especially for certain animals, such as birds.

Specifically, titmice; we're very social birds who nest together in both human and animal form.

When my parents disowned me, it was like they cut a piece of my heart from me and kept it for themselves. The people that were supposed to be there for me, love me unconditionally, and support me all my life said ta-ra without even blinking—and it really has nothing to do with my sexuality. I think they would have been ok if I had found another titmouse, but because Elise is a booby and I am a tit...*we're just star crossed-lovers.*

All those feelings of rejection, severance, and feeling so alone come rushing back to me as I stare at Arthur's uncle. My heart aches—it bleeds because I'm so scared that Arthur will be turned away in the same manner. I see how he looks at Belle. It's how we all look at Belle. She's something sweet, unique, and rare in our world. I hurt for him because Arthur's already given his heart to Belle, and I don't know if his family will be able to accept that.

Mine certainly couldn't.

Elise
THE BOOBY

Sian is squeezing my hand so hard I'm afraid she might break it. I quickly tuck her under my wing reassuringly and hug her to me tightly. I know what she's thinking. I can see it written all over her expressive, beautiful face. It's worry for Arthur and Belle, *for all of us*. Her old hurts and pains are coming to the forefront—for her parent's rejection and mine.

What Sian has failed to realize over the years is that my family's rejection, while hurtful, isn't something I didn't expect. Growing up, all prim and proper, my parents were always very cold and distant—I already felt detached from them. While their rejection was painful, it wasn't debilitating.

It was for Sian, though.

She had grown up in a family that was used to being affectionate. My family could barely give each other a civil greeting in the mornings. It's clear that Arthur is very similar to Sian and has grown up with a loving family. The lucky fellow has cousins, aunts, uncles, and more all living together in one place.

Truthfully, I'm jealous of Arthur and his family—even of Sian, who had a brother. My childhood was filled with imaginary friends and the ghosts of ancestors I never met, but hoped would have cared for me. As an only child, I had no one. Not even a nanny because my parents couldn't find a booby—and that's the only thing I have in common with Sian.

You don't seek friendship, help, love—anything—*outside of your species.*

At a very young age, you're taught who you are and where you stand in the shifter world. Unfortunately, blue boobies don't rank very high. In retrospect, it's as if my parents couldn't handle this, and so, they amassed ungodly amounts of money to lord over the one creature that would always be beneath them—*humans.*

Before I met Sian, my parents' wealth bought me everything. Private schooling, a coveted job position, posh clothes, you name it. Yet, the instant my parents found out about my relationship with Sian, I became persona non grata—*as if a titmouse is truly any lower than a booby.*

For weeks after both of our families cast us out, I contemplated breaking up with Sian. At least then, I know her parents would take her back in. It would take some time before they could mend their relationship, but at least my beloved would have her family back. Sian had no one but me—because *of* me—and I felt terribly guilty. I was used to being alone, but she wasn't. It was unfair and selfish of me to take that from her, but Sian wouldn't hear anything of it— she loved me, and we were together for the long haul.

Then, we found Jack, Theo, Jude, and Arthur.

We started our own family, and it became perfect when Belle joined us. Whatever happens here today—whatever Arthur's family decrees—he knows that we've got his back, and we'll support him no matter what. Shifter's Anonymous was more than just being the lowest man on the totem pole. It was about finding a place when we had been cast out, when we had nobody, when we were alone.

It was about finding family.

Shifters sneer at humans, but it is not I who pity them. They would pity us if they knew about our existence and our damning hierarchy that keeps us from truly loving. I look at Belle—so free and beautiful, embracing who she is, accepting who she is, as well as all of us—and I realize, Belle doesn't need to learn how to be a shifter now that she is one.

No, it's us shifters that need to learn how to be more like her—*human.*

Chapter 9

Jack
THE ASS

My cousin is the first person to say anything as we step off the train. It's pretty obvious who Dageus' father is as Arthur's cousin looks just like him. True to form, any time Harry opens his mouth, he makes a blunder of it.

"Howdy, I'm Harry the Arse, and I need a shower—some dude was riding me bareback this entire time, and I'm sure you can imagine how sweaty I am."

Dageus' father blinks, the stoic look never leaving his face. Belle pushes forward with a disgruntled look on her lovely face.

"*Really?!* He gets to say things like that, but *I* get yelled at for misconstruing things?!"

"Anyone who's a shifter doesn't get confused by things like this," I mutter to her.

"Well, that's just horseshit. Or donkey shit...or whatever kind of animal shit," she snaps, throwing up her hands.

Now, the clan leader slides a look over at her, something

unreadable passing through his eyes. Arthur hurries forward.

"Uncle Alastair, this is Belle—the one that we were telling you about."

"Aye, she's a lovely lass, indeed. Nice to meet you, Belle," he greets her formally.

Belle steps forward to shake his hand.

"Nice to meet you. I really appreciate you helping us. I know..." She trails off. "I know it's outside your comfort zone," she finishes as diplomatically as possible for her.

Alastair quirks a smile.

"That's putting it mildly, but we always help clan. Any friend of Arthur's is a friend of ours and part of our family."

At these words, Sian exhales a deep breath that she probably didn't even realize she was holding. I see Elise give her a hug before releasing her. Poor little birdy, I know what she was worried about. Hell, if we're all being truthful with ourselves, we probably all were worried about the same thing in the back of our heads. But Arthur wouldn't have taken us here if he thought it wasn't safe. His uncle might be displeased, but Alastair wasn't going to turn us away—especially *not* with all the things we have to tell him.

"So, how 'bout that shower?" Harry prods, slinging an arm over me. "Jack the Arse here could use one, too."

I roll my eyes, but chuckle.

Good old Harry—great for breaking the tension.

Alastair nods.

"Dageus, you have your Rover here and I have mine. We can drive everyone back home and get them settled. Afterward, we can have a belther[1]."

Dageus nods

"Of course, Laird, it will be done."

Even though it's his father, the bloke is super formal.

"Arthur, Belle, Sian, and Elise, why don't you come with me," Dageus directs.

I roll my eyes.

Great.

I'm going to have to sit in a car with Harry, Jude, and Theo. Theo's not so bad, but Jude and Harry don't get on. It'll be hard to keep Jude from choking him—probably even harder to keep the Laird from choking him—and I'm pretty sure my Aunt Millie would be upset if anything happened to Harry.

We're only children, and even though we're Primaries, we're higher up since we're larger mammals. But being mammals, well, you don't have as many chances to procreate when you're shifter like us. Parents tend to dote on their children because they're so rare to have—another reason why Sian and Elise's parents' rejection cuts them deeply.

Alastair drives us back to his house. Harry reminds him why we're the arse-end of everyone's jokes. As punishment for being his cousin, they room us together, and as my own personal form of punishment to the git—I beat him to the showers and use all the hot water. I chuckle loudly as his curses follow me down the hall and out of the house.

I spot Belle outside the large white house, refreshed in different clothing that fits her, staring over the lake that's gleaming in the sun.

"Penny for your thoughts," I prod.

She looks over sideways at me and smiles.

"Keep your penny; I'll tell you for free—I'm worried about Sian and Elise. Sian...she looks so sad. Do you know what's wrong?"

I cock my head.

"Have you asked her?"

"No...they've roomed together, and I didn't want to bother them. I didn't know if the question was too intrusive."

"Well, you're their friend now. I'm sure that they would tell you. It's not really my place to share, though," I answer.

Belle nods in understanding, and we lapse into thoughtful silence—me thinking how sweet she is that with everything on her plate, the Yank's still more worried about us.

"Tell me about yourself," I suddenly prompt.

Belle shrugs.

"Not much to know that you don't already. I'm American —from Nebraska—and I'm studying Lit at Oxford."

"Yeah, but *why* are you studying Lit?"

Belle crinkles her nose adorably.

"Well, I guess because I've always loved to read and thought there wasn't enough passion about classic literature. I mean, do you know how fucked up Shakespeare is?! Everything is an innuendo! Why is nobody appreciating that more?! As Benedick said in *Much Ado About Nothing*: I will live in thy heart, die in thy lap, and be buried in thy eyes. Freaking 'eyes' is an old word for vag! Only you Brits would liken eyes to fur burgers.."

I laugh.

"Of course, you would love Shakespeare. You two are peas in a pod. And trust me, you don't have to tell me what a perv Shakespeare is—*all* British children know."

"Well, they're not telling *American* children," Belle smirks. "In fact, I'm pretty convinced that my English teachers in high school had *no idea* what Shakespeare was really saying—like Georgia O'Keeffe's flower paintings... queef coughers all day long."

I choke at this, nearly dying.

This woman is too much, and I adore her.

"Queef coughers?!"

"Yep, every red poppy that woman painted was a ham candle warmer; just like most every covert sex reference Shakespeare makes is about some lady's calamari cockring."

If I didn't love the Yank before, I just fell head over heels.

"What about your parents? What do they do?" I ask, steering the conversation away from fannies.

"Dad's the regional manager of a chain of grocery stores and my mom is a news anchor."

"Oh, wow, that's aces," I say.

Belle shrugs.

"You couldn't pay me to do that job—the woman has to be at the studio at four in the morning so she can do the five o'clock news. No, thank you."

I cringe.

"I agree. It doesn't sound as glamorous anymore. No brothers or sisters?"

"Nope, just me, my mom, and my dad. I had a really happy childhood, but there wasn't really much to do. Like I said, I lived in the middle of nowhere. I went to the University of California, Berkeley for undergraduate school and realized that I just adored classical literature and decided that's what I wanted to get my degree in. Then, I was offered my scholarship at Oxford—*and how do you pass up Oxford?!*"

I roll my eyes.

"I know, right? Although, that *is* a pretty big accomplishment. You should be really chuffed for yourself."

"Chuffed?"

"Proud," I explain, and Belle beams.

"I am. Thank you."

"But what do you plan to do with your classical literature degree?"

Now, she frowns, and I want to kick myself in the arse for taking away her smile.

"Honestly...I really don't know. Initially, I wanted to be a traveling professor who teaches about what Shakespeare is really saying, but I don't know how many people would hire me when they find out that Shakespeare was actually just a bunch of porn poems."

Her words make me laugh again.

"Yeah, you might have your work cut out for you in the States, but you know, they do need Shakespearean professors here in the UK. Who knows, maybe one day you could teach at Oxford."

Belle snorts.

"Not as long as Dean Stiffdick is there. He's too uptight. Also, he tried to breed me—which is totally *not* cool."

I grimace and look away.

"No, that's definitely not *cool*." I look back at her and put a hand on her knee. "Are you ok? You know, we've been so caught up and on the run that I never stopped to ask."

For a moment, Belle's face is bleak.

"Yeah, I'm ok, but it was a close call," she admits. "If I hadn't gotten out of there...something definitely would have happened to me—they would have pinned me down and, ah, bred me."

For the first time in my arse life, I want to go against a Tertiary. Fuck, I don't want to just go after him—I want to murder the tosser to make him pay, even though he didn't succeed in breeding Belle, but because he tried.

It basically amounts to rape.

He tried to rape my sweet Belle—and succeeded in turning her into some monstrous creature.

"Don't worry," I reassure fervently. "We'll get even."

Belle gives me a wink.

"Oh, I plan on it."

"How's that?" I wonder.

"Oh, you know—you don't bite the hand that feeds you. In this case, it's the other way around. They created me, and I bite back—as does the tail coming out of my ass."

Her smile is still just as beautiful as before, but it's edged with something a little more sinister.

And fuck if it doesn't get my blood pumping.

She's a monster after my own heart.

Chapter 10
Belle

$\mathcal{I}$ sit there holding Jack's hand, touched that he cares so much about me. In truth, I really try not to think about what happened to me—not because I'm tucking it a way to ignore it so it can crop up later and cause me a mid-life crisis—but when I think about it, it causes a weird, burning itch inside me, the anger making me want to shift.

And we all saw what happened last time that happened.

So, it's just best not to even revisit that. Instead, I drink in the beauty around me. Oxford has some beautiful things to see, but this—*this is something I've never seen before.* It's breathtaking. Scotland is a beauty all of its own. It's rugged, untamed, and oh-so very masculine.

If Scotland were a person, it would be a man with the biggest dick on earth.

And if Nebraska were a person, it would be a flat-chested spinster who wouldn't know what to do with a dick if it slapped her in her face.

It's easy to revel in the vastness of Loch Kemp.

You might be saying to yourself, *But Belle, isn't that all Nebraska is—vastness?*

Yes, but it's just an expanse of *nothing*. Here in Scotland, the vastness is dotted with mountains that touch the sky and mysteries that are still left unsolved. There are no mysteries in Nebraska. Correction: we eat chili on cinnamon rolls, and that *is* a mystery.

"Your eyes are glazing over, love. Are you ok?" Jack asks with concern.

"Yeah," I murmur, "I'm still looking out around me. I'm just taking in this dick in my face kind of place."

Jack snorts.

"I literally never know what you are going to say."

"That makes two of us," I joke. "I've just never seen anything like this. It's beautiful here."

Jack looks around him.

"Yeah, it is. Did you travel much outside of Oxford?"

"No, I found I got myself into a lot of trouble with the locals."

Jack rolls his eyes.

"Considering how you don't understand a lick of what we're saying, I can see that. Well, when we get everything resolved, I'll have to take you home and show you around. Arthur isn't the only one who has beautiful things to show you."

My breath catches in my throat. I don't know what excites me more—that he wants to introduce me to his family, or that he definitely thinks we're going to get this resolved because that really just makes one of us who thinks that. I'll be honest, my current situation seems, well, insurmountable. But if Jack thinks that we can take down the bad guys, find an antidote to what's happened to me, and we'll all end up living in connubial bliss; then I am happy to follow in his footsteps because what I'm thinking is going to happen is *way more depressing.*

I think that the bad guys are going to start a war, have way too many people fighting on their side, and I'm going to die trying to fight them—except, I die because my ass bit me.

And by ass, I mean my tail that's a snake.

I hope everyone mourns me properly and sticks a dildo in my casket for me to use in the afterlife, just like the Egyptians did with their Pharaohs.

With this plan of attack, dying doesn't sound so bad now.

Jack tugs on my hair.

"What are you thinking about?"

"Death. I've got it covered." Jack just rolls his eyes. I nudge him with my shoulder. "And what about you? You made me talk all about *me.*"

Jack scoffs.

"I barely got anything out of you!"

"Bull! It's your turn to tell me about you."

"Brat. Fine. I'm from London, actually. My dad's a plumber and my mum's a schoolmarm—oh, and we're arses."

I giggle.

"Your dad's a plumber *and* an ass? Does he always have his sticking out?"

"Har, har," Jack says, "like we haven't heard that one before."

"Go on," I prompt, but Jack quirks a brow at me.

"I basically gave you the same amount of information that you told me about you."

"Nuh uh! I told you I didn't have any brothers or sisters." At this Jack winces. "Oh, what's wrong?"

"I had a wee sister..." Jack trails off.

"A little sister?"

"Yes, when I was younger."

"What happened?"

Jack looks significantly pained; so, I quickly back off and tell him that he doesn't need to share with me if he doesn't want to. But his face takes on a brave, stoic look, and he takes a shuddering breath before starting.

"No, you've told me things that are very personal; so, I can share with you. Do you remember what Theo told you about us? How, in the shifter world, you're born your animal and then shift into human form?"

"Yes."

"See, after that first shift, we can't transform into our animal again till puberty. It's a protection mechanism in our species—since children can't really control themselves the best—but my little sister, Angela, was different. Something was wrong with her; she started shifting immediately after she turned two. It was quite a shock for my mum and dad, and she had to go live out in the country with my aunt and uncle."

I can see the muscles tensing around Jack's neck and collarbone. Pressing a swift kiss to our connected hands, I wait silently for him to continue.

"I rarely got to see Angela, but I loved her. She was the sweetest thing, and my parents doted upon her so much. They planned to move to the country so we could be with her as soon as possible, but were waiting until my school year ended." Jack's hands begin to shake as he takes another deep breath. "Angela's favorite thing was to shift and chase lorries as they would go driving by my aunt and uncle's farm house. One day, when she was outside playing, she ran in front of one. It hit her and killed her."

I gasp, a hand flying to my mouth.

"Oh, Jack, I'm *so* sorry," I tell him with all the heartfelt sorrow I feel. "I can't even imagine how your poor parents or you handled it."

"Yes, it was very hard on all of us. As Theo said earlier, children are cherished because they're just so rare for shifters. There's so many extenuating circumstances that have to be in place for our kind to have babies. My little sister was a gift—a wonder—and her loss really affected my parents. They completely withdrew. It was actually Harry's parents who were taking care of Angela, and I'm closer with them—they're more like my parents than mine are. After Angela died, my parents just retreated into themselves. I spent my summers and most weekends with my aunt and uncle. It was great because Harry's only a year older than me; so, he's like a sibling—but it's not the same when you actually lose one. Don't tell Harry I told you this, but he was the one who was supposed to be looking after Angela."

I cringe.

"*Oh, no.*"

"I don't blame him, or anything," Jack hastily adds, "and I really hope nobody else does because we were just little kids ourselves. Eight year olds aren't really supposed to be in charge of four year olds—especially when that eight year old is, well, *Harry*. Sometimes I think he acts the way he does because he's trying to hide all the hurt inside of him."

Jack stares off into space, his shoulders slumped. I bump him with mine in a friendly manner.

"Hmmm, maybe. Or maybe he's just a perverted sex fiend like me for no reason at all."

Jack quirks a smile before relapsing into silence again.

"It's hard being a shifter," I whisper more to myself than to him.

"Yeah, it really is."

"You know, when I was a kid, my friends and I would play 'What kind of animal do you want to be?' I'd always pick something cool—like a mermaid."

Jack rolls his eyes.

"There you go picking things that don't exist again."

"Hey! What would be cooler than being part fish while still being part human?! I could eat tacos and swim—tell me that's not a win-win!" This makes Jack laugh, and I feel some of the tension ease around us. "What I was saying, though, is when you're a kid, it's just a game. So, you don't think of the ramifications of it. But nothing has ever been more serious to me than what's happening right now. I can't even imagine the kind of stress your kind constantly lives in —especially if you're a Primary. I just wish there was something I could do."

Jack nods.

"We've all been hoping that for all of our lives."

It's right then and there that I make a decision.

I'm *not* going to die on the battlefield with my ass biting me.

I'm *not* going down without a fight—*and that fight is to make things right for Primaries.*

Chapter 11
Belle

Someone clears their throat behind me making me jump up and spin around. It's Arthur and standing next to him is a man that is undoubtedly his father —they are absolute replicas of one another. Except Arthur's father is older, and his hair a little bit grayer and darker. Interestingly, both wear the same solemn looks. Before Arthur can say anything, his father slants him a frown.

"I thought she was *your* sweetheart?"

At this, Arthur blushes, and I bite my cheek to keep from smiling.

Nothing makes me want to jump a man more than when he blushes.

It screams, 'Take control of me and make me your bitch'—but only in the best way.

Like where I'm wearing leather and he needs a safety word.

"Da!" Arthur exclaims, "I didn't say she was my girlfriend."

"Well, good, because she looks like she's *his* girlfriend."

I realize that Arthur's dad thinks this because I was holding Jack's hand and quickly rectify the situation.

"No, sir, you have it *all* wrong—I like your son's dick *and* Jack's. Er, I mean, I like all dicks—*not your dick, though!* Ugh, sorry, that sounded bad. I'm sure your dick is great, but I think that would make things awkward. What I really meant to say was we're all good friends, and we all like each other."

"Wow," Jack murmurs under his breath.

"Wow," Arthur echoes.

I sigh.

"Didn't quite stick the landing on that one, did I?"

"No," Jack laughs. "Not at all."

"Let's start over, Mr. Arthur's dad. I'm Belle," I greet, sticking out my hand.

Arthur's dad never loses his solemn look, but there's a twinkle in his eye as he steps forward to shake my hand.

"I'm Phineas. Nice to meet you."

I smile, relieved the guy's willing to overlook my social faux pas. Also, his name is Phineas, which makes me think that he might have a platypus named Perry hidden somewhere, making me love the man even more.

"Arthur tells me you're in a right bit of trouble." I shrug in answer to him. *That's putting it mildly.* "Why don't you come inside? The clan elders have all gathered and we're here to listen about what's going on."

I nod, wondering if it's safe for me to speak after what just happened.

Clearly, Phineas thinks the same thing because he whispers to Arthur, "It might be best if you explain."

The three men lead me inside where a group of elderly Scotsman have gathered. There's five of them in total, and they remind me more of hobbits—*and one of them is defi-*

nitely trending on the Gollum end. His skin is almost like leather, and it's bumped up with warts.

"What's going on with him?" I whisper to Arthur.

"Oh, that's just Graham. He's going to die soon."

Arthur says this so nonchalantly my mind barely comprehends his words. When I do, I skid to a stop and just stare at him.

"What did you say?"

Arthur halts and comes back to me.

"Sorry, love, sometimes I forget you're not one of us. So, we're born our animal and we die as our animal. As we get closer to that death, our body slowly shifts back into our first form. And then..."

"And then?" I prompt.

Arthur shrugs.

"And then you croak."

"Is that a horny toad joke?!" I demand, not amused.

Arthur bites his lip but Jack and Phineas are openly smiling now.

"That's not funny," I grouse, pushing past them. I walk up to the five men. "Hi, I'm Belle, nice to meet you."

The clan elders all garble out what I assume is a greeting, but it's hard to understand because their accents are so thick. I'm not even sure they're speaking English. I decide somebody will fill me in with what's going on when Jude, Elise, Sian, and Theo step into the room, followed by Harry, Dageus, and his father, the Laird.

"Jude has told me most of the details, as well as Arthur," Dageus' dad begins solemnly. "We are now just waiting to hear what you have to say."

"Eep!" I squeak. "I thought I wasn't supposed to talk?!"

Peeking over at Phineas, I see him cover his mouth with a hand—the man is most definitely laughing at me.

"Maybe keep your love of cock to yourself," Jack advises under his breath to me. "We don't want to give anyone here a heart attack."

I scowl at him.

"I'll have you know that I can go a good ten...er, five minutes without thinking or talking about cock!"

Elise and Sian have come to join me at my side.

"Only because you're thinking about poon," Sian teases.

Damn it, she's got me there.

But I'm going to prove them all wrong.

I've got this.

I clear my throat and stand before the elders.

"What is it that I need to say that Jude and Arthur have not?"

Hopefully, it's not very much; that way I don't stick my foot in my mouth this time.

"You're most assuredly human?" one of the elders asks me.

"Yes, I mean, I was until Doctor Fuckf—I mean, Doctor... I really don't remember his name. Let's just stick with Fuck-face. It's *more than* applicable. So, as I was saying, Dr. F-Face injected me with something."

"But you're positive before that—"

I cut him off.

"Dude, I'm a grown woman. Don't you think I would know if I were a shifter?"

The old man shrugs.

"Sometimes there are anomalies in our kind."

At this, Harry and Jack shuffle uncomfortably, probably reminded of Jack's sister who shifted too early. It makes me wonder if there are some shifters who *can't* shift.

But surely that can't be me because my parents would have said something, right?

58

Also, I mean, if my parents were shifters, it would be pretty obvious to me I would think.

I doubt my mom and dad could hide something like that. I was *the nosiest kid* on the face of the earth. I always knew what I was getting for Christmas months ahead. (In my defense, my parents were *terrible* at hiding things.)

"No," I answer the elder. "There is *no* way I was anything but human before this."

He nods.

"I understand. It's just something we had to consider. That being said, this changes everything for the worse."

And it absolutely does.

If I had been some rare anomaly in the community whose blood not only makes me a breeder, but I was able to turn into a shifter because I latently was one; then there probably wouldn't be anything to worry about too much—except for the fact that I'm some type of monster.

But this is far worse.

It's the fact that anyone injected with the shot can become a monster.

Do you know how many idiots there are in the world who are just waiting to become monsters?

Stupid ass folks—like the idiot who posted on social media about his heists—who can turn into lions with venomous snakes and dumn billy goats coming out their back end...

Does that sound good to you?

Now, I don't want to be the Debbie Downer here, but honestly, it sounds like the Tertiaries have won before the war's even started!

I answer more questions, and eventually, they ask me about the breeding—that thankfully never happened. I fidget uncomfortably, not really wanting to recall it, but knowing I need to be as honest as possible to help. When I finally get done, Graham looks at me with hazy eyes.

"Then, it is as we have feared," he announces. "Humans and shifters are co evolving together."

"What does he mean?" I ask through the side of my mouth to Arthur, not sure if I understood him correctly.

"I mean, lass, that shifters are so endangered humans are changing to accommodate us. When a species is endangered, it either goes extinct, or it finds a way to survive. In our case, it's finding a way to survive. There can be no other explanation. If a human woman can carry a shifter baby, it is because evolution is pushing us towards survival."

With these words, the elder suddenly just disappears.

His clothes go floating to the ground while I scream and point, but Dageus' dad walks up calmly to the clothes and pulls out a limp toad.

Looks like Graham just croaked.

Chapter 12

Theo

THE SLIPPERY DICK

"Prepare the fire—we're having frog legs."

Belle screams at the Laird's announcement.

"We're going to eat him?!" she screeches. "What the fuck?! Cannibalism is not cool!"

"I'll take her outside," I volunteer, grabbing onto her hand and tugging her away.

She's still shouting when I finally get her out of Arthur's uncle's house.

"Belle, love, calm down."

"How can I calm down after hearing something like that?" she hisses.

"They're not going to eat him," I explain. "They're just going to burn him."

"Like that's any better!" she shouts.

"How is it any different from cremation?" I wonder, holding up my hands.

This shuts her up.

"Oh, good point."

"We have to burn our dead—ignore that pyres are simply a Scottish ritual—this is our way of honoring and commemorating the one who has passed away. But I promise you, they're not going to eat them—there's nothing *to* eat. He's probably already turned to ash."

Belle snaps her mouth shut and gets a thoughtful look on her face.

"Oh, yeah. I remember you guys saying that to me once about when you die."

"Yep. No matter how we die nor what type of shifter we are—including Tersh, Secondary, or Primary—you turn to ash as a way to ensure our safety. An evolutionary mechanism as Graham would've told you."

"I hate that," Belle says. "I mean, I guess it's handy and all for you, but I just hate how it's like you never existed."

"I understand. It's just the way it needs to be for our kind. And we know we existed and you know we exist," I say softly with a smile at her.

"I guess I kind of overreacted in there, huh?"

"Hey, don't beat yourself up. You didn't say anything about trouser snakes."

She chokes on a laugh.

"Yeah, I guess there is that, huh?"

I walk her out back towards the lake.

"Jack said you really liked it out here."

"I do. It's so beautiful and peaceful. I can kind of forget everything for a moment looking at all that's around me."

"It's something special, huh?" she murmurs, gazing at the lake. "Hey, you wanna go for a swim?"

"No," I swiftly negate "I don't."

"I mean as a human, not as your fish."

"I would need to ask Arthur if it's safe first."

"What the hell's in Scotland's lakes that it's not safe to swim in it?!" Belle exclaims, side-eyeing the body of water.

"Well, this *does* drain from Loch Ness, and we all know what they say is in there."

She squints.

"I don't think this is big enough to have something the size of the Loch Ness Monster in it."

"Do you really want to test it?"

"Well, when you ask me *that* way—no."

"Sorry, love, I *always* have to be cautious. It's something that was instilled into me since I was a little boy. If you get eaten as a slippery dick...that's it."

"You know, I was reading and thought that slippery dicks could only come from the ocean."

"The majority of my kind are salt water fish, but I'm a very rare freshwater species."

"Oooooo, special," she teases.

I smirk.

"It does make it easier. There's some shifters that have to be in either freshwater or saltwater if they want to shift, but I can go in both."

"I suppose that is handy," she says. "Do you go to the ocean often?"

"Actually, no, I've never been. My parents—they're terribly fearful. If you can get lost in the lake; imagine what can happen in the ocean."

"Yeah, I can see how that would be worrisome. There's just some things I never thought about before."

"When you're shifter, you have to look at life in a completely different way and ask yourself, '*Is this going to kill me?*'"

Belle cringes.

"That's a terrible way to live life."

I shrug.

"If we want *to live*, it's how we have to be."

"I wish I could change *everything*—I *am* going to change everything!" she murmurs with conviction.

The certitude in her voice makes me smile. There's not a doubt in my mind if this woman says she's going to do something that she's going to succeed.

Suddenly, Belle bends forward and clutches her stomach.

"Ooooh!" she moans. "It burns! There's a terrible burning in my stomach!"

I quickly jump up and yell, "I'll get someone for help."

"I'm not horny! It's not horniness. Usually, if I feel a burn, I think I'm horny."

She's muttering this to herself, and I dash off to get the others. I burst back into Laird's house, where the others are still conversing after Graham's death.

"Help!" I shout. "Something's wrong with Belle. She says she's burning in her stomach!" Immediately, Jude and Jack push past me and rush out. I chase after them, followed by Arthur, Harry, Sian, Elise, Dageus, Alastair, and Phineas—I'm sure the elders are hobbling along, but we're much faster and arrive back to Belle before them.

The sight that greets me when I get back down to the lake is one I will never forget until my dying day. Belle is running and screaming, the sound so shrill and high it freezes the blood in my veins. She's sprinting in circles, making a mad dash to escape the black mamba that has shifted on her body.

"Oh, god!" Elise gasps. "She spliced!"

My stomach drops as the mamba nearly bites her. All of us stand frozen, not sure what to do. The snake strikes again, and I can't hold myself back. I sprint forward, without a plan of attack, intent on saving Belle. The lovely Yank comes to a halt upon seeing me—the mamba does, too, and instantly poses to strike. It rears back to bite me just as Belle slams her hands on her hips.

"Oh, no, you fucking don't!" she snaps at it. "If you bite my friend, I don't care how much pain it'll cause me—I will cut you off and feed you to the sharks!" Belle pauses in her tirade. "Anyone here a shark shifter?"

My mouth hangs open, and nobody answers her because I know that they're all in the same type of shock I'm in. *Splicing is dangerous and painful.* It's when a shifter's stuck between their animal form and their human form. More often than not, they can't find a way to shift back completely to one form or another and have to be put down like animals—*the pain is so great they usually beg for it.*

Of all the terrible things that can happen to my kind, I think this is the one I fear the most.

Yet I realize Belle wasn't screeching from pain, but her fear of the snake biting her—*a snake that she now has complete and total control of.* I watch in wonder as it shrinks down and coils docilely behind her. She starts to flap an agitated hand at it before I quickly command her to quit.

"Stop!" I hiss in a hushed voice, making everyone look at me now like I'm a radge[1]. "You're going to rile the mamba back up—you're in control of it right now," I explain.

"I have a hole in my jeans!" Belle cries.

I chuckle.

"It's ok, love, we'll get you new pants. For now, we need to figure out a way to retract your snake."

"I don't even know how it came out!" she exclaims before another look of terror washes over her expressive face. "Oh, my god, is it, like, coming *out of my ass*?! I mean, I don't think so...but I don't know. Is like the tail end in there?

65

I don't feel anything...I mean, I walk around with butt plugs a lot, though; so, I'm kind of desensitized back there."

"Jesus," I hear Jude mutter.

"My kind of girl there," Harry grins.

"She's *not* your girl," Jack mutters.

"What's a *butt plug*?" one of the elders asks, and I just put my face in my hand.

I don't know if the shifter world is ready for Belle.

Chapter 13

Belle

*O*k, I think, *don't panic—this isn't the first time you've had something long, black, and scary in your ass.*

My mental pep talk does little to alleviate the fear of having a snake coiled against me. Nothing is scarier than having one of the most venomous creatures on Earth attached to you—*literally*. At least the things not attached to me via its fangs, right?

Aside from that fact, it's hard to find anything positive about the situation.

"How do I get rid of it?" I whisper, hoping not to agitate the deadly thing.

"You've got to shift back into your human form completely, lass," Phineas tells me.

"I don't know how to do that."

Everyone facing me cringes, giving me very little hope that the situation is going to get any better any time soon. Thankfully, there's Jude—beautiful, pragmatic, stalwart Jude—who comes to my aid.

"You're just going to have to learn how to shift and control it."

I nod at his sensible answer that sounds easier said than done.

"Right, I can do that—tell me what I need to do."

He pauses and looks around to the others, a little help-less. They give him the same look in return as if they cannot verbalize how to shift. Albeit depressing, I *do* get it.

If you've been doing something your entire life, how would you explain to somebody how to do it?

How would you explain to somebody how to breathe—take in big puffs of air and puff them back out?

It's just something innately that you do. It's not some-thing I've ever thought to explain to another person. I mean, you can puff the air in and out—doesn't mean that the oxygen is getting to the lungs. You can tell me how to shift, but it doesn't mean that I'll be able to do it. Still, a gal's gotta try because my other option is to walk around spliced—and spliced is *not* my jam. I think this is one of the few times I would've taken the goat instead of the black mamba. Buuu-uuuuut, if I ever get this splicing shit down, I can do badass things like splice just a lion head but leave the rest of me human. You know, like a mermaid. Sort of. Where mermaids are half-fish and half-human—I'm half-lion and half-human—but the *top* half of me is the lion.

O.M.G.

I'm like the progressive commercials where the guy is half motorcycle, half human!

I'll never laugh again when I see those on TV; I'm also going to have to switch my loyalties to Geico now.

We half breeds have to stick together.

"Are you thinking about shifting?" Arthur prompts.

"No, I'm thinking about car insurance," I answer truthfully, making Jack laugh.

"Focus, love. This is pretty important."

"Well, I'm waiting for the instructions!" I snap right back before quickly quieting my voice. "Oops! Do you think it's upset?"

I peek behind me to see my snake is still coiled docilely against the small of my back, but it has an eye open—*and it's trained on me.* Taking a deep shuddering breath, I give it the same look right back. The beast needs to know who's the alpha between us.

Between you and me... it's the snake, but we don't want the snake to know that.

I turn away before it can call my bluff.

"All right, tell me how I can become fully human again. It's going to be pretty hard to hit on someone with a snake coming out my back end."

Phineas looks confused.

"Why's the lass going to hit someone?"

"Obviously because of what they did to her!" his brother, the laird, supplies.

"No—'hit on' means to... ah, wow. I've never had to define this. To express your sexual interest in someone?"

"She means 'to tell someone that she fancies them'," Jack explains before turning to frown at me. "Why would you need to be "hitting on" anyone else?!"

I snort at his possessive tone.

"You heard Beyoncé—*you* didn't put a ring on *this*. 'Til then, I'm a free agent and I'll wink at whoever I want to."

"*Wink?* Is that what they're calling it nowadays? And it's a little bit more complicated than that, don't you think?" Jack parries.

"Not really—all you have to do is ask me to be your girlfriend."

Jack runs a hand through his grayish-brown hair and looks away.

"I didn't think you did boyfriends and girlfriends, or anything like that."

Now, I slam my hands on my hips.

"Excuse me?! Just because I'm a fiend of... er, sexual deviancy doesn't mean that I can't commit! Is that what you think?!"

Jack finally stares back at me, a little sheepish.

"Actually, yeah, that's exactly what I thought."

I suck in a breath and hear an angry hiss behind me. I swivel around to see the black mamba rising up; its baleful glare trained fully on Jack.

"No, no, it's ok. We're not mad at him—well, we are—will you just go back to sleep?" I snap at the scaley menace.

The snake hesitates before receding back down, coiling into the crook of my lower back once more.

"Woah!" I whisper. "Did you guys see that?! I'm like a snake charmer!"

I see the gang looking suitably impressed at my talents.

"You have formidable control of your animal already, lass" Phineas praises, and I smile, proud of myself.

"At least we won't need any antivenom immediately—but we probably need some just in case. All right, Jude, help me. Tell me how I can shift back into being human."

"You know," the laird of the clan starts, "it might be better for you to shift into your animal and then shift back into being human."

I shudder at the thought.

I really don't want to do that, and he really doesn't want that to happen.

Arthur tells his uncle as such, but the man just shrugs.

"This isn't something we've ever seen before. Any of our kind that's ever been spliced hasn't been able to act like this—they're in acute pain. How to tell her to shift from one form to another is not something that I think we can articulate to her, but she might recall becoming her animal more readily."

"Well, can someone please try to explain!" I plead in desperation. "I'm not going to be able to go anywhere like this!"

"How did it feel when you first shifted?" Elise wonders.

I think back to the boat before answering.

"It was burning and painful—like something was trying to get out of me. But I didn't feel that this time! I was just sitting here; then—BOOM—all of a sudden I felt a poking sensation as something ripped out my pants and was a man-eating snake."

Theo raises a brow.

"It just happened? What were you thinking about?"

I pause, wondering.

"Well... I was upset—*am upset*—about how Primaries are treated, and how shifters feel like they have to live their lives. You know, that you all think humans would be such a threat. Everything is so much more difficult for your species —*but especially for Primaries*. I don't like how you're treated and the thought enraged me."

Arthur nods sagely.

"This is why your snake reacts to your anger then—it came out *because of* anger."

"So, my snake is my volatile emotions trying to escape? Sheesh, the creepy bastard is making it really hard to box shit up."

"No, your animal is just your animal," Jude interjects

with a smile. "It came out because it thought you were threatened—it didn't realize you were just upset for us. Your snake meant to protect you, but because you reacted the way you did, the mamba thought *you* were the threat. But when it knows you're in charge—"

I nod, interrupting him.

"The creepy fucker calms down! I guess I *am* the Alpha! Huh—didn't see that one coming."

With this awareness, I feel more in control. Closing my eyes, I try to recall shifting. I remember the feeling of fur poking through my skin, the sensation of my bones creaking and contorting to change shape...

Suddenly, my eyes fly open when I realize that I'm recollecting how to shift into an animal—*not into a human.* At the moment, I can't even bring to mind how to be *a human.*

And not remembering your humanity is the last thing you want when you turn into a man-eating lioness.

Chapter 14
Belle

A loud rumbling sound fills the air, and it dawns on me that it's *my stomach.*

I'm hungry.

Heck—I might even be *hangry.*

Human Belle didn't need food, but Chimera Belle might.

Now I know exactly how that shark in *Finding Nemo* felt when he smelled Dory's blood.

Just like he was having 'fish tonight', I'm having human.

Of course, I *can't* have human though—they're my friends—and do I really want that weighing down my conscience?

I'm still feeling pretty guilty about seducing my third grade teacher and his wife—*not* while I was in third grade, though (just in case you're wondering how messed up I am).

With the grace of a ballet dancer with a goat coming out of her ass, I spin around and run into the darkening evening. I gallop along the bank of the lake until it trickles into a little stream. I follow it until, all of a sudden, I almost fling myself headlong into a large body of water—at least ten times bigger than the one back on Alastair's land. I remember the Laird saying that Loch Kemp connects to Loch Ness.

Was this the infamous body of water that everyone spoke about that supposedly harbored some monster?

I peer down into the inky blackness of the liquid, trying not to make out my own reflection, convinced of the monster that I'll see there. Ripples in the water catch my sharp eye, and I realize I can see much more than I could as a human—it's almost like having night vision. I can also sense the creature moving underneath the water.

My heightened senses allow me to smell it, too. Except, it doesn't smell like a fish, though. How I even know this is beyond me. My animal brain must know things I do not know.

The ripples in the water keep getting bigger and bigger. I raise a paw, edged with sharp claws, ready to swipe at whatever jumps out so that I can eat it. But instead of being a small aquatic animal to dine on, a flipper bigger than my entire body comes out. Another quickly follows, bracing itself on the bank in front of me as I scramble back, squeaking out a shrilly lion roar.

A head rises from the water, followed by a neck so long I wonder if Scotland harbors some unknown species of water giraffe. I don't have time to contemplate this because the creature lunges at me with lightning speed. I fall once more onto my goat, who screams in pain, before I shift painfully.

Like the last time, I lay there panting—naked, cold, and now terribly frightened.

At least before I had a snake coming out of my ass that could bite you, inject you with venom, and kill you to protect me.

Now it's just me, *human Belle.*

The only thing I have going for me is that I'm a great squirter—but this really doesn't seem like the time and place for something like that... unless I could quickly make myself orgasm and spray the water monster in the eye, maybe blinding it for a moment to get away...

But honestly, I'm just not in the mood.

The water giraffe's large head is inches from my face, and the thing definitely looks like it could be a dinosaur. I really wish I had a camera for Dean Unbendableprick; so, he could see that dinosaurs are clearly *not* extinct. Just as quickly as the creature appeared, it dips back into the dark depths of Loch Ness, blending into the murky shadows perfectly.

Like an idiot, I quickly scramble up and peer over into the water. This time, when something pops out of the water, it's my *human* scream that pierces the air because it's not the water monster from before—*it's a man!* I fall back once more on my ass. Like a pro swimmer, the dude pushes out of the water and vaults up until he's lying between my spread, naked, wet thighs. His dark head dips down as he licks between them. I gasp in affront—and if we're going to be honest with each other, maybe a little arousal. It's hard to see now that I'm not a lion anymore, but the stranger is ripped and hot—and he's licking me between my thighs. So, I'm going to cut myself a lot of slack for my not-so-very logical response to him.

"You taste delicious," the stranger growls in a thick brogue.

Now, I'm concerned that he actually might want to eat me, but *not* in the sexy way.

"I taste terrible!" I squeak.

The man's nose bumps my clit.

"Nae, lass, anything that smells this good can't taste bad."

Suddenly, I'm not convinced he's talking about eating me for dinner. A long drag of his abrasive tongue right over the center of me quickly rectifies any confusion my brain might have been having over his words. All thoughts flee from my head—but my body... *it jumps right on board.*

"I'm Nestor, and I'm claiming you as my mate."

The guy barely raises his head to make this rather scandalous announcement.

"Erm... no thanks," I decline as politely as possible.

Nestor finally eases back between my legs to prop himself up on his elbows to look down at me. We're both naked, and the whole situation is really shaping up to epic levels of awkwardness.

"Why not? Are you already mated?" he demands. He sniffs me before I can answer. "You don't smell mated."

It makes me wonder what 'being mated' smells like—obviously, it doesn't smell like getting fucked because I have to *reek* of that.

I clear my throat.

"I'm *kind of* mated."

Nestor raises a brow at this.

"*Kind of mated?* I don't think there can be such a thing."

"It's complicated," I hedge.

Nestor snorts.

"It's *not* complicated. Whoever your mate is, I will fight him and kill him. Then, I will claim you as my mate."

Now, I look at the wacko like maybe I need to get away no matter how amazing his muscular body is.

"Hold up!" I command, throwing up a hand and forgetting my plan to escape. "*Him?* What if my mate's a woman?"

The stranger's brow furrows in confusion like he's never contemplated this before.

"Well, I guess I'll fight her to claim you as my mate?"

"Are you asking me or yourself?" I laugh.

Nestor scratches his head, too hung up on the problem of my mate potentially being another girl.

"Listen, don't sweat it. I can't be your mate, anyway. I'm not... whatever you are... OH MY GOD!" I screech as realization slams into me. "You're the Loch Ness Monster!"

Nestor scowls.

"We don't like being called that," he asserts, making my eyes widen.

"There are more of you?!"

"Of course, there are more of us, lass! Well, nae very many, though," he admits sadly. "Actually, only one more, and if we don't procreate soon, there will be no more. What luck that I found you on my banks—a creature different like myself. I can smell you, my mate, and you call to me in a way no one else ever has. It doesn't matter that you're not the same as me. We're compatible." The certainty in his words brings me back to what Dr. Fuckface said—maybe I do have some kind of special blood that allows me to be a breeder for any shifter.

Even the legendary Loch Ness Monster.

Chapter 15

Jude
THE COCKCHAFER

The sound of Belle's scream nearly makes me drop out of the air. I shifted the instant that she ran, but my cockchafer is not nearly as fast as her chimera—*and that's saying something.* I know she's heading towards Loch Ness and hearing her lion roar really unsettles me, but her human shriek stops my heart.

I fly as fast as I have ever flown, beating my wings rapidly in the hope that I can get there in time to save her from whatever has frightened her. If it's as she's feared and her snake has bitten Belle, there will be nothing that any of us can do— we won't be able to get the antivenom in time. *She'll die.*

I push myself past the point of exhaustion and finally— finally—I spot her, but not as I dreaded. She's not withering to death because of fatal black mamba venom. Instead, what greets me is an equally horrifying sight.

A naked man lying between her very naked thighs—*and the git is licking her.*

I see red, which is an interesting concept because my cockchafer can only see in black and white. I shift midair, falling to the ground in a crouch that I instantly spring out of. Sprinting towards Belle and the strange man, I prepare to tackle him back into the black waters of Loch Ness, but the wanker lifts his head before I strike. Something feral crosses over his face. He pushes off Belle before jumping into the shadowy waters of the lake. Without thinking, I prepare to dive in after the bastard, but Belle grabs my arm to halt as I pass.

"Jude, stop! It's not what you think."

Before she can say another word, a huge, lumbering mass rises from the inky liquid in front of me, making me gape in shock.

"I-i-is that... no, it can't be!" I mumble incoherently, but Belle nods.

"Yes, it's the Loch Ness Monster."

The creature has two flippers perched up on the bank in front of us. They're larger than a double decker bus, and the thing's neck is nearly five meters high. Its head is large and the mouth is edged with sharp teeth lethally spiking out of it.

I start to hyperventilate in the presence of such a rare Tertiary, but bravely tuck Belle behind me with the intent of protecting her from it. The monstrous thing growls at me as a large tail comes out to wrap around Belle and pick her up. She shrieks into the night.

"Nestor! Put. Me. Down!"

I realize she doesn't sound scared, really. In fact, she just sounds downright peeved.

"Nestor?" I blurt out.

"It's his name," she needlessly explains before continuing, "but I'm going to call him 'Nessy' if he doesn't put me down! Hear that, Nessy, you big brute? Put me down!"

In response, the Loch Ness Monster just shakes her.

"That's it!" Belle roars. "I'm puking on you!"

Instantly the aquatic beast drops her back onto the bank. Belle coughs from having the wind knocked out of her by the motion.

"Are you all right?" I ask solicitously, helping her up off the ground.

The Loch Ness Monster has transformed once more into his human form, and before Belle even answers me, she swivels around to punch Nestor right in the bollocks. The man howls in agony, and I step back, cupping a hand over my own manhood. I wince in sympathy, even though the bloke doesn't deserve any. It's around this time that all the others finally catch up with the Laird leading the pack. Everyone came in their human form. Alastair blinks in shock at the sight before him.

"Nestor, is that you, my boy?"

The man groans painfully in answer.

"You know him?!" I question furiously.

"Aye," Alastair confesses. "He's one of the only two remaining niseag."

Harry stares at the naked stranger in fascination.

"The creature is real?!"

"As real as any shifter," Alastair answers gruffly. "But unless you're an elder, we don't say anything. They prefer their privacy—not to mention there's only two of them left."

"And we're going extinct!" Nestor moans. "If I don't claim the lass here as my mate, my kind will die."

"Well, you just can't go around claiming chicks as your mate!" Belle snaps at him. "I understand the plight you're in... sort of... not really. *But still*, you can't just be like, 'hey, wanna bone?' I mean, I guess I do that all the time..."

She claps her own hand over her mouth to shut herself up, and I stifle a laugh.

"What is the lass talking about now?" Phineas demands.

"She's my mate," Nestor claims with conviction.

"She can't be," Phineas denies. "Belle's not a niseag."

Nestor just shrugs.

"I can smell it—she *is* my mate. We were meant to be."

Arthur's dad runs a hand over his neck and looks over at him.

"Son, your lass has got a lot of competition."

"There's no competition!" Belle interjects. "Can't we all just... I don't know, *share*?!"

I cock my head at the idea.

In the shifter world, you have one mate, depending on your species. Sharing really isn't our thing. Not to mention the rarity of finding another of your kind that you connect with. Still, in our case where there's a scarcity, it would make sense to share. In fact, some animals around the world do this because of the few females available.

I frown, thinking of Nestor's words.

He says that Belle is his mate—*that he can smell it on her.* While I've always scented something different about her— unique, even—it wasn't that she was *my mate*. I remember Belle saying something about the other Tershes smelling this, too.

Is there something special about her that only Tertiaries scent her as a mate?

The idea sits sideways with me because it reinforces that Primaries are nothing and Tershes are something superior —that Belle, perhaps, is superior, and I am not. Of course, I know she's something rare, but my heart aches with the truth that we were never meant to be together.

I can see this by the look on Phineas' face.

Arthur's father knows that to be the mate of the Loch Ness Monster is something prestigious—something singular—certainly not meant for his son.

And unquestionably not meant for me.

Chapter 16

Belle

"Perform the ceremony!" Nestor booms to Alastair.

"What ceremony?" I demand.

"The one for our mating bond," the insane man clarifies.

I throw my hands up in the air, even more exasperated than before.

"You can't just claim me as your mate! You act like you peed on me or something!"

"He peed on you?" Harry calls from the back. "What kind of kinky fuckery are you into?"

"Not that!" I interject. "I mean, even I have some hard lines, and I draw them there. I don't do any type of excrement, but I am into getting tied up."

Nestor quirks a brow.

"You want me to tie you up to have sex?" he drawls slowly, like it's a novel idea that has never crossed his mind.

"Yes, er, I mean, no," I answer. "I mean, *yes*, I like to be tied up for sex, but *you're not* tying me up to have sex because we're *not* having sex... because I'm not your mate."

I don't think the man hears a single word that I'm saying.

In fact, I'm very, very convinced that he's just envisioning tying me up and screwing me.

I would be lying if I didn't admit the thought crossed my mind for a split second—just the barest hint of an image before it was dashed away with the reminder that I'm not bonded to this guy. *Who, for clarification, is a total and complete stranger, not to mention the Loch Ness Monster.* Huffing a sigh, I walk over and take Nestor's hand, prepared to let him down gently. He squeezes it, and before I can say anything, looks deeply into my eyes and whispers words in a language I've never heard. I assume it's Gaelic. Unfortunately, I have no clue what the handsome psycho is saying.

Alastair steps forward and puts a hand over where Nestor's and mine are joined. Arthur starts to say something, but Phineas promptly shushes him. I see him give my horny toad a meaningful look that Arthur seems to get. Whatever it means must be depressing a.f. because my favorite Scotsman looks ready to cry.

The Laird sighs heavily before nodding solemnly. Nestor copies his move, and then both men look at me. It's like the weirdest, non-sexual three way I've ever had. I would totally be lying if I said I have any idea what's going on. I stare down where we're all holding hands, trying to figure what the fuck is happening. Nestor clears his throat and gives me a pointed look.

"You have to say, '*aye*'," he instructs.

"I?" I repeat confused.

Do they mean I like me or eye *like my eyeball?*

"Or do you mean 'aye, aye' like a cap—"

"No, love!" Arthur shouts, but I can tell by the look on his face that It's too late.

I wait for something terrible to happen—for me to shift

back into my creature, or for Nestor to change back into the Loch Ness Monster, or maybe even one of the asshole Tertiaries after us to jump out from behind a bush.

But nothing happens.

I wait a beat, standing there, still holding hands with two men I just met. Of course, this isn't the first time I've held hands with strange men while naked. Usually, shit's progressed past this point, though. Considering my new reality, I really need to start carrying clothes around.

At least Alastair has clothes on.

Seriously, I want a relationship with Arthur, but every holiday I spend with him will be so awkward now that his father, uncle, and cousin have seen me nude. There needs to be a way for shifters to have clothes accessible right after they change back and forth. I bet I can make a fortune if I could remedy that. Then again, I've noticed that shifters are really comfortable being naked, and that's something I can get behind. I always felt I should've lived in a nudist colony.

Arthur's murmur and the growls of the other guys around me are what snaps back to the present. Jude and Jack look fit to be tied. Theo looks like somebody stole his puppy. Sian and Elise look worried. Even Harry looks a little peeved. Dageus just seems to be watching everything unfold, and Arthur is wearing the same depressed look from before.

"What's going on?" I ask just as Nestor wraps an arm around my waist, bringing our two very naked bodies in sync with one another.

"We are now joined," he crows in delight.

I stare at the bizarre guy. He's really shaping up to be the strangest Scottish dude I've ever met. I'm beginning to think he hasn't spent much time being human and understands nothing about normal interaction. Like, just because our hips are touching doesn't mean we're *joined*... huh, maybe he doesn't *really* know what sex is.

"Maybe he's a virgin," I whisper to the others as if they've been privy to my mental ramblings.

At this, Nestor scratches his head.

"Why do you think I'm a virgin?"

"Because you just said we were joined, and *clearly*, we're not. I mean, our hips are touching, but we're not joined in the way like your penis is balls-deep in my vag."

"I didn't mean we were joined *sexually*, lass, I meant we're *bonded eternally*."

"What?!" I squeak.

Arthur sighs.

"I'm sorry, Belle. I should've spoken up before, but Nestor made a verbal claim for you as his mate. To challenge him would mean to fight him... and a horny toad is not going to win against a niseag. You solidified the bonding pledge when you said *aye*."

"No, no, no, no, no. I said *eye* like eyeball... or did I say *I* like me? Either way, I didn't mean it! Besides, now that I think about it, I was asking whether it was like 'aye, aye, captain'!"

"Aye means yes," Alastair interjects.

"No, it doesn't!" I deny hotly. "It doesn't count if I'm not speaking in your dialect!"

"It counts," the Laird corrects. "I'm sorry, but you bonded to him."

I throw my hands out.

"That's illegal! It can't be legal to do that! I want a lawyer. You can't possibly make me be his mate just because he whispered some words to me in a language that I didn't understand. Clearly, I didn't know what was going on. Don't you have laws here in this country?"

Phineas nods.

"We do, but we also have laws for our species that super-sede human laws. They're binding—just like your bond with this man."

I cut a vicious glare to everyone in the group.

No one has prepared me for the shifter world at all.

Chapter 17

Sian
THE TITMOUSE

*B*elle's face is turning the same purplely shade as her hair, and I'm wondering if we should be concerned. I look to Elise, who is glaring daggers at Nestor, but none of us here will ever go up against him. He's one of the rarest, most powerful Tertiaries on the face of the Earth. Certainly, no Primary would go against that—*not unless they had a death wish.*

But I can tell by my girlfriend's face that she's absolutely livid on Belle's behalf. Quite frankly, I agree. What the Scotsmen did was diabolical. Poor Belle, who was never meant to be a shifter, has been thrown into a world where she has no idea how it works. Of course, none of us have had the time to explain anything to her, let alone something this life-altering and severe.

Mating bonds are unbreakable.

It creates a permanent link between the two shifters that can only be broken in death. Wisely, none of us volunteer that information right now because there's a chance that Belle might just actually kill Nestor.

Actually, by the looks on their faces, there's still a chance that Jude or Jack might.

But maybe this solves all our problems...

Arthur fell head over heels for our Belle—Theo, too—and there's no doubt that Jack and Jude feel the same way about her.

Would they have been able to share?

There's just no way of telling, and it could have very potentially torn us all apart.

So, maybe, it's best that Nestor has claimed her. Except, Belle doesn't seem like she's ready to settle for that. She's still screeching about illegalities. When Nestor reaches up to tweak one of her nipples to silence her, the feisty Yank punches the randy Tersh right in the meat and veg. Nestor crumples to the ground once more. I see all the other guys wince and cup themselves, but Elise and I lose it.

"Definitely don't tell her about the 'death do us part' clause," I whisper to Elise, who chuckles.

"No, Belle's angry now, but she would never kill anyone. She wouldn't harm a fly," she argues.

I look from the Yank back to my girlfriend and raise a brow.

"If she can maim his knob, I'm sure she could kill him—we all know how much Belle loves dick."

Elise seems thoughtful at this.

"Hmm, maybe you're right, but let's convince her to kill him *after* the war."

Nestor is still writhing on the bank of the lake, groaning in pain. Somehow, he manages to grunt out:

"What war?"

Startled, I realize he was listening to us the entire time. I straighten up.

"The war with the Tershes."

The plonker doesn't say anything as he takes a few seconds to collect himself. Finally, he rises from the ground and takes a healthy step away from Belle.

Smart bloke.

"What war with the Tertiaries?" he demands.

"It's a long story," Elise sighs, "but suffice to say, the Tershes are taking humans and using them to experiment on and to breed—humans like Belle, who obviously is now a unique shifter."

At this, Nestor gnashes his teeth together before foolishly stepping back into Belle's personal space. He stares down at her from his great height, easily over half a meter taller than me.

"I will not let that happen. We will fight them together. Do you know why?" he demands of our Yank.

"Because it's the right thing to do?" she postulates.

"No, because I am your mate," Nestor corrects.

At this, Belle arches back and decks him in the junk again.

"For the last time, I'm not your mate!"

Elise
THE BOOBY

The journey back from Loch Ness to Alastair's house is a

solemn one where Belle and Nestor are split apart. At the rate he's going with the Yank, the man won't have to worry about ever reproducing because she'll have castrated him on her own.

Not that I can blame her.

I would be furious if somebody bonded to me in such an underhanded manner. I can tell by Sian's face how worried she is about the others and for Belle. I worry about Belle, too, but she's strong—she won't take any shit from anyone. But the others... I worry for them. Arthur and Theo are so tenderhearted. Jack hides his pain behind a facade of jokes, and Jude is so solemn and serious. Belle brought out the best in him—out of all of them.

The beautiful woman managed to bring them all out of their shells. Unfortunately, I can see them all retreating back into them now that Nestor has claimed her—but I understand why Alastair did it. Nobody here is going to stand up to a Tertiary—*let alone the Loch Ness Monster*. He's a powerful man that you don't want to *not* have on your side. At the end of the day, the Laird cares less for Arthur's feelings than he does for the safety of his entire clan—and turning the Loch Ness Monster against your entire family isn't the wisest thing to do—not to mention the war where we could definitely use some Tersh strength.

But it's all so bloody unfair.

I want to scream.

For Belle, who never asked for any of this to happen to her.

For the boys, who just want to have a relationship and be normal.

And for Sian and me, against the cruel unfairness of a world we live in.

When we make it back to the Laird's house, the Elders

are still there, waiting. They bow down to Nestor, already knowing who and what he is without being told. Then again, they're older than dirt and outdate Nestor. The Tertiary regally nods back. I can tell the man doesn't spend much time in human form, but he definitely knows that he's at the top of the food chain around here. Dageus's mum runs around muttering about preparing the master bedroom for him. Belle slams her hands on her hips when she hears.

"Why are you giving him your bedroom?!"

Dageus' mum stutters to a stop.

"He is newly bonded... you are newly... I-I-I thought you would both enjoy the larger chamber," the harried woman stammers.

"You know, to consummate your bond—" one of the Elders begins, but Belle just arches a savage brow.

"If one more person talks to me about mating this fuck—"

Nestor quickly strides away from her, placing a hand over his crown jewels.

"Please stop mutilating me, lass," he interjects in a pleading tone. "I'm the last of my line. Well, if you don't include my grandfather, but do you really want to mate with him?!"

"I don't want to mate with any of you! You never asked!"

"Lies!" the Tersh roars. "I can smell you—and you want to mate with me."

"Ha! Has it even occurred to you that I always smell horny?!" Belle bellows.

At this Nestor blinks.

"Yeah," she sneers spitefully, "you're nothing special. I smell this way for little old ladies who walk by me on the street!"

At this declaration, Dageus' mum pales.

"I'll just go check on the room," she whispers, slipping away hastily.

"I didn't mean you! I'm not horny for you!" Belle yells out, making us all laugh.

"Will somebody please go tell her we don't want your bedroom and that I *don't* want to boink her," she begs to no one in particular.

"It's a great honor to be offer—" the Laird begins.

"I know it's an honor," Belle interrupts. "Listen, where I come from, it's rude to take someone's room like this. I understand you're just trying to be hospitable, but you're only doing it because you think he's the Loch Ness Monster."

Alastair stares at the Yank.

"Lass.... he *is* the Loch Ness Monster."

"Yes, I know he is," Belle huffs. "What I'm saying, though, is he doesn't deserve any more special treatment than the rest of us. We're all equal—just like I assume you don't think you're any better because you have a penis and I have a vagina."

Alastair appears thoughtful and opens his mouth to say something, but Arthur quickly shushes up his uncle.

"Belle, love, this is a different time and different era than my uncle and dad grew up in," he attempts to rectify. "How about we just all go in for the night and get some sleep?"

I stifle a grin at his redirection of the conversation.

"Yes, that sounds like a wonderful idea," Nestor purrs, sounding like Harry.

Belle looks like she's ready to deck him again when, suddenly, a sinister smile wreathes her face.

"You want to mate with me?" she demands of the Tertiary.

Nestor's eyes light up gleefully.

"Yes, I do; although, we are already *mated*."

"Well, if you would like to finish the mating bond, I have a stipulation."

Nestor nods eagerly, ready to agree with anything to slip between her thighs—not that I blame the bloke.

Belle has some pretty lush thighs.

"If *you* want to mate with *me*, then I need to bond with Arthur, Theo, Jack, and Jude, too."

"What about me?" Harry cries, making me snort.

"Down, boy. One arse is enough for her," I tease.

Although, if anyone could handle more, it would definitely be Belle.

Chapter 18

Theo

THE SLIPPERY DICK

We all gape at the outrageous Yank, but I don't know why we're surprised by anything that Belle says anymore. Granted, this isn't nearly as outrageous as it sounds for the sheer fact that she simply just doesn't understand how shifters mate. I run a hand through my blonde hair in agitation as I try to explain this to Belle.

"Is it because your mom and dad aren't going to see the wedding?" she wonders.

I laugh.

"It's not a wedding. It's something different... more profound and *permanent*, depending on your species. Although, my mum would love for me to have a wedding. She's Irish—very Catholic and churchy—but my dad's North Irish."

"I thought the Irish hated the North Irish and vice versa," Belle says with a crinkle of her adorable nose.

"Eh, they have a love-hate relationship," I smirk. "Besides, things are different when you're a shifter—your

95

animal identity comes first. Arthur here is a little bit different. I've noticed that he and his clansmen put their ethnicity first before their shifters."

Belle hums thoughtfully.

"So, you're a slippery dick before you are a North-South Irishman?"

I nod, trying not to chuckle.

"Yes, that's how I see it—I'm a fish first."

"Right. Well, I guess we'll just have to tell your folks that we eloped to Gretna Green!" she jokes, and I roll my eyes.

"We can't mate, love. You're *already* mated—to Nestor."

Belle scowls.

"That was not of my choice! I was tricked into it, I say, tricked! Besides, if I can mate with the Loch Ness Monster when I'm *not* a Loch Ness Monster, then it stands to reason that I can mate with any of you."

I look over at Arthur, Jude, and Jack, who all just kind of shrug because the brilliant Yank has a valid point. Nestor stands there with his arms crossed, unamused. I don't know if he's upset because he hasn't consummated the mating bond with Belle yet, that she keeps punching him in the junk, or because she's demanding that she mate with the rest of us.

If I were to be given a guess, it would probably be the latter—*but the Tersh can't really be angry at us for Belle's ultimatum, can he?*

I shudder. He probably can, and being a slippery dick makes me *especially* afraid of water predators—the last person I want to piss off is the Loch Ness Monster.

"Well, tell me how we can make a mating bond so we can just do it. All Nestor did was say some words with Alastair holding our hands together. Give me yours and mutter the same words," she snaps.

"What if they don't want to be your mates?" Nestor throws out.

Belle's face blanks, and it's obvious that she hasn't even thought of this. She turns to us in surprise—and guilt.

"I'm so sorry," she starts. "I didn't even think about any of you *not* wanting to mate with me..." Her anguish over the idea is palpable, and I quickly put a finger to her lips.

"I would be *honored* to be your mate," I say with the heartfelt sincerity I feel inside.

Jude steps up to her right side, Arthur to her left, and Jack steps up to her back. Together, we envelop her in a hug as the three all avow how wonderful it would be to have someone as special as her as our mate. I know right then and there that none of us care if we had to share Belle because it's better to have some of her than none of her.

"But," I explain, pulling back a bit, "mating ceremonies are different for all shifters."

"Well, what are the words that slippery dicks use?" she prompts.

I shrug.

"My kind doesn't really use words because we complete the bond while we're in fish form. Obviously, there's... *you know*..." I clear my throat in embarrassment when the woman who put herself in sexaholics anonymous looks clueless. "Sex...a mating bond involves sex, but there's so much more to it. As I mentioned, it varies from shifter to shifter. Slippery dicks are required to be in our shifted form because we rub our scales against one another."

Jude nods.

"Cockchafers have a similar ritual. For example, we fly around and spray each other with our scents."

Belle frowns.

"Well, I suppose you could do that to me... but don't you

97

dare get too close and get stuck in my hair! But if I shifted, I don't know what I could spray you with besides venom or lion pee... Ooo, maybe my goat could spit on you!" she offers.

Jude shudders.

"No, thanks."

"I don't understand," Belle states in blatant confusion. "What did Nestor say that made me his mate that we all can't do together?"

Arthur steps up to explain.

"Nestor didn't actually use the niseag mating bond; he used the old Gaelic wedding ceremony to claim you as his mate. Your mating bond will be complete when you..."

"When we fuck," Nestor finishes crudely.

Belle points an aggressive finger at him.

"You hush up, Buster! We're not doing any boning any time soon!"

Nestor gives her a look that suggests she better change her mind quickly, *or else*. This raises my hackles, and I turn to glare at the Tertiary.

"You better not hurt a single hair on Belle's head! And if she says no—"

Nestor steps up into my personal space.

"What are you going to do about it, little fish?" he sniffs.

But before I can even answer, Belle is squeezing in between us, stabbing Nestor in the chest savagely with her finger.

"Don't you call him a little fish! He's a magnificent, beautiful, slippery dick, and I love him!" she professes softly.

Nestor's eyes enlarge at the same time mine do.

"You love me?" I gape, completely gobsmacked by her confession.

Trying to be nonchalant, Belle shrugs.

"Well, you know, I love all of you—you four are pretty easy to love. The truth is, you all need it so badly because your fucked up hierarchy has made you its bitch. Your world says you're not good enough, but not me. I see how special, wonderful, and unique you all are. I love that you have always accepted me, always supported me." Belle turns to look at Nestor as she continues. "I don't care if everyone says the mating bond is unbreakable—if you can't see them as equals, then we will *never* be anything together."

The Loch Ness Monster gnashes his teeth together, clearly not used to being told what to do, but Belle isn't budging. *Well,* I mentally amend, *she's wiggling a little.* Purposefully, too, I think. Her arse shimmies against my aching dick, making me wonder if this is conscious or subconscious. *Even when being serious, the Yank's a little tease.*

Jude places her hand on my shoulder, pulling my attention away from my rapidly tenting pants.

"Give Nestor time. You have to understand that we live in a different world—a very prejudiced world, I admit—but we've been raised to show deference to him as he's been raised to look down on us. It'll take time to change that."

Belle gives the Tersh one last glare.

"Well, if he ever wants anything from me—even as simple as a friendship—he better figure it out quickly." She turns to Arthur, "Where is your uncle so we can do the mating ceremony?" Arthur chokes.

"I told you, lass... it's just not that easy."

"Well then, we can at least just do the consummating part!" Belle grabs my hand. "Come on, Theo, let's go!"

I look over at the others in shock, not really understanding what the hell just happened.

If I'm not mistaken, I think it's about to be my wedding night.

Chapter 19

Belle

I lead Theo upstairs to the bedroom given to me by Arthur's family. My slippery dick seems a little tense, and I realize that I am, too. Clearing my throat, I make this confession. Theo's eyes widen.

"Why are you tense?"

"Because I haven't orgasmed in over a day—that shit is seriously unhealthy for you!"

Theo chuckles.

"Should we, uh, rectify that?" he offers shyly, and I could just eat the man up.

"Yes, please," I purr. "Let me slip into something more comfortable.

With the subtlety of a stripper, I take off all my clothes before pushing Theo down on the bed and lying down on top of him. His breathing is fast and erratic.

"Er, Belle, I don't really know how to do this..."

"What?" I ask, baffled. "Fuck?"

Theo swallows thickly and looks away, his blond hair covering his expressive green eyes.

"I'm a virgin," he mutters in embarrassment.

I feel my jaw drop at his words.

"A virgin?" I whisper in delight.

Theo nods.

"I love virgins," I breathe.

"You... do?"

"Yeah—well, I love anyone, really, but I get off to the look of amazement on someone's face when they first experience ecstasy with another person."

Theo bites his lip, and my south mouth starts drooling.

"It might be... quick."

"I like quickies!" I reassure. "Sex is like pizza—it's good cold, hot, two days old, whenever! Besides, if it's quick, that just means we can do it again. And again. And ag—"

"I get it!" Theo laughs. "So... how do we start?"

"First, you need to get naked."

Theo slowly rises off the bed and begins nervously pulling his shirt over his shoulders. His skin is pale, and I can see the greenish veins under it as well as the firm muscles. I lick my lips and wait for him to keep going. The tease unhooks his pants, but takes his time removing his socks and shoes. Finally, he yanks down his pants and boxers. I fall to my knees in front of his beautiful cock, begging for attention.

"I'm not very big..."

I snort.

"That's what you have a fist for."

Theo blanches, and I burst into laughter.

"Kidding! Besides, haven't you ever heard 'it's not the size but how you use it'?"

"But we've already established that I don't know how to use it!"

"But I do—so, we're both going to enjoy it."

With this, I pop my mouth over his cock and shut him up. I love the sweet, salty taste of his jizz mixed with his sweat. I suck my mouth over the tip and feel him shudder.

"Belle! I'm going to—"

He doesn't finish, but rather explodes inside my mouth.

"Mmmm," I hum in satisfaction.

Is there anything better than getting someone off?

Theo is coughing and trying to move away from me, ruining my post-BJ bonding I was doing with his bologna pony.

"I'm so sorry. I can't believe—"

"Theo!" I shout, gaining his attention. "*Stop.* I'm not judging you. You have *nothing* to apologize for—this was just round one."

Theo expels a breath.

"Round one?"

"Yeah—and you finished in record time!" I tease with a wink. "Now, let's move onto round two."

"Ok... round two. How many rounds do you usually do?" Theo asks tentatively.

"Sex is like a marathon—you have to practice and build up stamina."

"So, how long?"

I tug Theo to the bed, push him back down again, before seating myself in his lap and *on* his dick. Reflexively, I squeeze my vag around his thick girth, eliciting a groan from the sweet man.

"Do you know Lionel Richie?"

"Erm, sure..."

"We're going to do it like him."

"How does Lionel Richie do it?"

I kiss Theo long and deep, thrusting my tongue to duel

with his before pulling back to bounce up and down on his dick and answer:

"All night long, baby."

Chapter 20

Jack

THE ASS

"She can't be any of yours mate—she's my mate!"

Nestor grumbles this under his breath for what seems the fiftieth time, and I smirk at the naked, annoyed man. Nobody tells him to get some clothes on—because he's the Loch Ness Monster—but I think it's hilarious that the git's sitting here in the buff, scowling about wanting his mate when she's naked with somebody else. I'm not particularly afraid of the Tertiary; at least, not when we're this far away from water. So, being the peach that I am, I decide to egg him on some more.

"I think Belle made it very clear that she doesn't want to be your mate—she'd rather be ours." Nestor cuts me a hostile glare.

"Then, why aren't you up in that room with her?" he snarls.

I give him a feral grin.

"Because we've already fucked," I tell him bluntly.

Just like that, I find myself pinned on my back, and the Tersh on top of me. He's wound his hands around my neck before I can even retaliate. Harry shifts into his arse and kicks his hind leg squarely into Nestor's chest, effectively knocking him off of me. I quickly scramble to my feet, this time more prepared, thinking that at least Harry's useful for something. But Nestor isn't attacking again—he looks almost stunned. The hoof print stamped on his chest is damned comical.

"You could have killed me!" Nestor roars at Harry, who's still in arse form.

My cousin brays in exasperation and rolls his eyes. It turns out the Loch Ness Monster is nothing but a sook[1]. It's then that Belle's breathy moan pierces the air—I would know that sound anywhere.

Any man would know that sound.

It boils the blood and hardens your dick quicker than morning time. Poor Nestor looks like he's going to go insane. I decide it's time that we took a walk outside before the sad bloke combusts. Maybe the cool night air would help clear his head; as well as the fact that his mate doesn't want to be his mate.

Oh, and that she's shagging someone else.

"Come on, Nestor. Let's take a walk. We have to talk," I declare, holding out a hand to help him off the ground.

Harry looks at me like I'm insane, but I wave him away. I help the Loch Ness Monster clamber to his feet, and I drag him out of the house, away from the intoxicating sound of Belle coming. Truthfully, I need to clear my head, too. It's hard to think when images of fucking her arse keep permeating my mind.

"My mate speaks of a war," Nestor finally says when I make no attempt to talk.

"Like you never could've imagined," I answer. "And our Belle is at the center of it."

Nestor's quiet for a moment.

"That... really doesn't surprise me," he jokes after a minute, and I chuckle.

The bloke's only known her for a few hours, but clearly he understands that Belle is some kind of chaos that works. So, I tell him about the other Tershes and what they've done to Belle. Even in the dark, I can see his face filled with rage.

For him, it does not matter that Belle was human—it doesn't even matter that she's now a monster—*none of it matters.*

Because in Nestor's head, Belle *is* his mate, and he's willing to do anything to protect her.

This alone is a consolation because the truth is, the rest of us aren't strong enough to fight the Tershes—not alone and not even together—but Nestor is. He's ruthless and fierce. Of course, all of this is contingent upon him being near a large body of water, but even then, he can still be on land for a limited amount of time.

Either way, I wouldn't fuck with him.

"I must go tell my grandfather this," Nestor announces.

I nod in understanding, and he goes racing off towards Loch Ness. I watch him make a graceful dive into the water before he disappears beneath the dark liquid. Turning back around, I follow along the stream that links Loch Ness to Loch Kemp. I don't go too far because I risk hearing Belle again—which was seriously disturbing knowing how many others are at the house.

Hopefully, everyone has left except her and Theo.

I grin, thinking of my blond friend—lucky Bastard probably doesn't know what to do with himself right now. Our

Belle is a kinky wench, and if you're not prepared for that, it completely takes you off guard.

But I'm sure Theo's adapting just fine.

My arse ears are more finely attuned to sound; so, I strip and quickly shift—*not* because I want to hear Belle's breathy moans, but to see if she's done.

And maybe to see if she wants me to join in...

But instead of gasps of pleasure, my ears pick up on splashing in the distance behind me. It must be Nestor getting ready to return to the house. Wondering where Harry is—probably glued to Belle's bedroom window, wanking it—the faint sound of voices on the wind makes me pause. They're coming from the lake, and I wonder if it's Nestor talking with this grandfather.

Did the ancient Niseag actually shift?

Curious, I very quietly walk back towards the massive lake. Peering through the brush, I can barely make out the shoreline where Nestor is standing. In front of him is a man who blends in with the darkness of the night. I realize I *know* this man—it's not the other Loch Ness Monster.

It's the Secondary Jackal that attacked us back at the port.

My arse ears strain to pick up their conversation. The wind snatches at the words, blowing them sometimes to me, but mostly away. I hear the word *fight*, *enslave*, and then *rule*. It doesn't take a genius to figure out what the Secondary is telling the Tersh. He's recruiting Nestor—*for his war*. Nestor is nodding, as if in agreement, and I want to race out and smack him.

Doesn't he know this is one of the men who hurt Belle?!

I see Nestor hold out a hand; the Secondary puts his out to shake, too. At this, Nestor's lips curl into a sinister grin. He pumps the jackal's hand up and down, as if in agreement, before letting out an ear piercing whistle. The Secondary winces, as do I, my ears flattening to the side of my head. All of a sudden, a form comes lunging out of the water; the enormous head attached to it opens its gaping mouth to snap around the arsehole jackal. The creature swiftly pulls the Secondary under the water, leaving nothing but ripples behind.

Holy fuck.

Grandpa Loch Ness just ate him.

Chapter 21
Belle

My post-coital bliss is interrupted by the braying of a donkey outside my window.

Hee-haw, hee-haw!

It's like a terrible serenade that makes you wonder if Jack is trying some ass-y way to get laid. I walk over to the window, open it up, and peer outside into the night. The cool breeze flows in to caress my bare skin. Theo comes to stand behind me and hisses:

"Get some clothes on!"

"Maybe Jack wants to see me see me naked," I parry.

"What if it's Harry?" Theo counters, making me frown.

He's right—I can't tell those two apart in donkey form in this little of light.

"Bray twice if you're Jack," I command to the animal below.

At this, Theo laughs.

"Do you really think if it was Harry, he'd tell you?"

Good point.

The donkey rectifies my problem by shifting into his human form—it's definitely Jack.

He most certainly was serenading me, and by the way his skin flute is standing at attention, he *definitely* wants to get laid.

Visions of me being the Pied Piper of Jack-flute dance through my mind...

"Quick," Jack cuts into my fantasy, "we have a problem! Get down here."

Just like that, he shifts back into a donkey. I look back at Theo helplessly.

"Why did he turn into an ass?"

"He wants us to ride him," Theo explains. "Something must be terribly wrong."

My heart rate starts accelerating, wondering what's happened. I look back down at Jack, waiting for me to get on his back. I'm a good two stories up, about twenty feet from him...

Jack just wants me to jump?

It really doesn't seem like a good idea, but when his donkey brays at me in urgency, I take a leap—literally—of faith. Behind me, Theo bellows. The sound startles me. I scream and tumble ungracefully out of the window. As I plummet below, something catches me. I'm still screaming; so, it takes me a second to realize that I've spliced again.

This time it's just my goat's head coming out my lower back—its horn is hooked on the window sill, miraculously stopping my fall.

I crane my head to look at it just as it does the same. Our eyes connect, and like the animal whisperer I am, I let out a shriek.

I scream.

You scream.

The goat screams...

Where the fuck is my ice cream?!

I'm totally going to need some after this.

Somewhere below me, I hear Jack yelling that it's ok and he's getting help. I snort out a panicked laugh.

How do you help someone in this situation?

I can only imagine what I look like dangling helplessly with a goat head sprouting from my body, its giant horn caught on the window sill keeping me from falling and breaking every bone in my body.

"It's ok, lass!" a familiar voice calls. "We'll catch you if you fall."

It's Phineas, Arthur's dad.

I look down and see that the clan Elders are with him. Where had *they* come from? Did they live with their Laird? In the room, I hear Arthur with Jude, Harry, Dageus, and Alastair. Everyone is here to witness my humiliation.

Can this get any worse?

I feel a tickling sensation on the inside of my thigh as something runs down it. It falls down below, and I hear a muttered curse.

"What the hell is *this*?" Phineas roars.

I swallow thickly because I know it's slippery dick jizzle.

Yep—it definitely can get worse.

There's no way I can date Arthur now; our family holidays have left the realm of awkwardness into a new dimension of mortification. I can easily envision it in my head...

"Excuse me, Mrs. Arthur's mom that I swear I don't want to bone, can you please pass me the gravy that looks uncannily like the sperm juice I dripped on your husband's face while hanging naked out your bedroom window via my goat's horn?"

I might end up a skanky spinster at this rate.

It takes *five* grown men to haul my grown-ass back in

through the window, mostly because my goat is screaming and trying to bite them.

It's kind of a jerk.

I tell it as much, and the fucker tries to bite me!

Well, I'll tell you what—I will *not* stand for this kind of behavior. The little bastard is like an errant kid who needs to learn his place. So, I punch it in the face because it's a goat, not a kid... I mean, it *is* a kid because *kid* means baby goat...

"Ahhhhhhhhh!" I howl in pain the minute my fist connects with the creature's ugly mug.

It's like punching myself in the face.

The pain instantly shifts me back completely into my human form. My chest heaves up and down from the exertion. I'm telling you this whole shifting shit is not for the weak. It seriously takes a lot more stamina—kinda like sex. People underestimate that shit, but you have got to be one limber whore to get into some of those positions.

Seconds later, Jack, Phineas, and the three surviving Elders come barreling into the room. Sian and Elise follow with Arthur's mom. Le sigh... when they say '*clan*', it must mean no privacy. Everyone is talking at once, and finally, I raise my hand.

"Jack, what's wrong?" I ask him.

He stares at me incredulously.

"Why did you jump out the window?!" he demands.

I shrug.

"I thought that's what you wanted! You were braying at me, and it seemed pretty damned important!"

"It is important—but not 'jumping out of a window' important! You're a chimera—you can't fly!"

His words make me snort.

"Thank you, Captain Obvious. Well, thank god my horn hooked me. Now, tell us what's going on!"

"It's the jackal—he's returned."

My body tenses up at his words as I envision the Secondary that attacked us back at the harbor. Before I can ask any more questions, Jack adds, "The other Loch Ness Monster ate him!"

This effectively shuts me up.

If I had any doubts about Nestor's loyalties, I guess I don't anymore.

"Everyone get dressed." Alastair commands. "We'll all go to the loch together."

I nod and slip into something less revealing—which actually isn't that revealing because it's not mine.

I think the dress must be Arthur's mom's... it might have some slippery dick cum stains on it.

"Your wife's gonna wanna wash this later," I mutter to Phineas as I walk out of the bedroom door. "It's dirtier than Monica Lewinski's clothes after her stint in the Oval Office."

Arthur turns red and just palms his face; Theo turns even redder. What he's embarrassed about, I have no clue, because he's not the one dripping baby batter all over the place—although it's *definitely* his fault. I give him a wink because I don't want him to feel guilty.

I enjoyed every second of being his cum dumpster.

The trek back to Loch Ness is even darker than before, and I do not enjoy it at all. Even though I'm surrounded by people with heightened senses, I don't trust mine. Hell, I don't trust my world anymore, not with what I've learned. When we finally come to the small clearing that leads to the lake, I see Nestor standing there, but he's not alone.

An older gentleman is there as well as the Secondary— he hasn't been eaten, but he definitely looks wounded.

Nestor's face lights up when he spots me, and he gestures to the bloodied man on the ground.

"A gift for you, my mate," he crows proudly.

I crinkle my nose at the man.

Did he just give me a dick?

Chapter 22

Belle

"*I*'ve just had some slippery dick in me; I'm good, thanks."

Nestor scowls at my polite decline, and I wonder if I've offended him by rejecting his gift.

"I don't sleep with people I don't know," I try again before I realize that's an absolute lie. "Actually, I totally do that. I get off the most to that shit."

I realize everyone's listening to me, and I'm talking out loud. The jackal dude is staring at me with big, pleading, wide eyes—he must really want me to screw him.

"Listen, you have a big, beautiful, black cock—and I love it—I'm just kind of overwhelmed by dick at the moment. Wow... I never thought I'd say those words," I mutter mostly to myself.

The Secondary's eyes just keep getting wider and wider. Finally, Jude steps forward, chuckling. "Nestor's not offering you him to shag, love," he clarifies.

"You're not?" I ask the Loch Ness Monster.

Nestor shakes his head.

"No!" he says with disgust. "I'm offering him to you for revenge!"

"I thought the older one ate the douche!" Jack mumbles somewhere from behind me.

"He is a gift for you," Nestor continues. "To use for information and then to torture at your leisure."

I throw my hands up in the air.

"Who the fuck gives a gift like that?" I demand.

Under his breath, I hear Theo whisper, "As opposed to him giving the bloke *to fuck*?"

"Hey!" I snap. "That's actually the perfect gift to get me! Please, gift me with things to cram into my taco shell."

Phineas frowns sternly at Arthur.

"Do *not* get the lass that gift!"

I wag a finger at him.

"Don't tell him what to do! You're ruining my surprise Christmas orgies!"

Arthur raises a hand to silence us all.

"We need to ask him questions to see who he's working for."

"I already told you who he's working for—Dean Rigid-wiener and Dr. Dieandgotohell."

"Yes, but we need to make sure that they're the masterminds and not working under someone else. Then, we need to figure out where they're at."

"Right. Okay, mister," I growl, making my voice as deep and intimidating as possible. Jabbing a menacing finger menacingly at the bleeding Secondary, I demand, "Tell us where Dr. Fuckface and Dean Stiffdick are, or I'll cut off your dick and smack your face with it!"

Everyone gapes at me.

I stare back, nonplussed.

"What? I thought we were threatening him?"

"*Not* by cutting off his knob," Jack sighs.

"Er, sorry. Let me try again... tell us where Dean Stiffdick and Dr. Fuckface are, or I'll smack *my* face with your coc— no, that's not right either. Guys, a little help."

"Just tell the git you'll bite him with your black mamba and kill him," Harry suggests, making the jackal man shudder, his eyes filled with trepidation.

"Yeah, bet you didn't know about that," I grin. "Dr. Fuckface turned me into a killing machine!"

"He wasn't supposed to know about that, lass!" Alastair moans, before chewing out Harry for even bringing it up in the first place. "Now, we surely have to kill the man—he knows too much."

The poor guy blanches at this assessment, and I kind of feel bad for him—even though he attacked us and probably wanted to do terrible things to me. Not to mention the terrible other things he might have done to other people. Ugh, the laird is right... the dude knows too much. I walk over to the Secondary and crouch down, but Nestor quickly pulls me back out of the jackal-man's reach. Rolling my eyes, I elbow the Loch Ness Bully off of me.

"Listen," I say, addressing the bad guy, "you *have* to tell us where the dean and his evil, stupid henchmen are. We can't let them do what they're doing—it's terrible! I have a goat and a snake coming out of my ass!"

At these whispered words, the man strains to look behind me.

"Not now, I don't!" I huff in exasperation. "But sometimes I do. And I'll tell you, a lot of people don't know how to handle big, black things in their ass like I do. I guess I'm just gifted like that."

"You said that she's on scholarship at Oxford?" I hear one of the Elders mutter.

"Yeah, that's what Arthur said," Phineas whispers. "Do you think the lad's lyin' to church her up?"

I turn around with my best WTF look on my face.

"You know I can hear you guys, right?!"

Phineas grins at me.

"I'm surprised you can hear anything over your own thoughts," he teases.

I scowl darkly at him.

"I'm going to have a Christmas orgy in your living room if you keep it up!"

My words wipe the smile right off of Phineas' face because I think he knows I'm absolutely serious. I look back at the man laying on the ground.

"Where are Dr. Fuckface's and Dean Dickler's head-quarters?"

Surely it wasn't where they had taken me before... that place seemed like a slap-together, last minute operation—and Dean Dickler didn't really seem like a slap-together kind of guy, ya know? The Dean of Douchecanoes definitely had a base somewhere. The jackal shifter hesitates finally before confessing:

"The Isle of Man."

An island of men?!

Sign me the fuck up.

I hear Arthur's sharp intake of breath and watch him run an agitated hand through his red hair.

"That's where the English wolverines live!"

"A what?" I demand, looking back at him.

"English wolverines—they're endangered and known for their ferocity and strength—especially in comparison to their size. It's been documented that they can kill other animals many times larger than their body size. And if the dean's headquarters are there—the wolverines are *definitely* shifters."

"What's going on at that island?!" I growl at the Secondary.

"The doctor's facility is there... together with the dean, he's creating new shifters. But beware—the island is guarded by the most vicious Secondaries."

"Chihuahuas?" I whisper.

The guy looks at me like I'm stupid.

"Hey! Have you ever been in a fight with one?! They're tiny, but mighty! I do *not* recommend messing with them."

"For fuck's sake, wolverines guard the island—obviously! Chihuahuas are just useless Primaries!"

My world goes red with rage.

I *hate* the bastard who sees everyone around me as worthless—it doesn't matter if they live or die.

I think it's time to teach this asschap a lesson in the value of life.

Chapter 23

Arthur
THE HORNY TOAD

"Go ahead and eat him."

Belle makes this command cheerfully to the older Niseag. He's in his human form, and it's probably the first time he's shifted in four or more decades. The elderly Tersh doesn't even blink at her words, just shifts right back into his terrifying beast. He opens his massive mouth to do as Belle's bid, making the Secondary screech in fright.

He gets up to run away, but Nestor just arm bars him across the throat, knocking the git right back on his arse where he belongs. I look at Belle in shock—this is so *not* like her. She's such a gentle, kind person but the look of steely determination on her face tells me that she's serious. As the older Loch Ness Monster clamps huge jaws around the Secondary, prepared to swallow him whole, Belle shouts at him to stop. The Tersh spits him back onto the ground where the Secondary manages to shift, despite his wounds.

Nestor quickly comes and kicks him in the side. The

jackal yelps and tries to take a vicious bite out of the younger niseag, but stops when the older one bares his teeth in warning. For some inexplicable reason, he's listening to Belle, and I'm not quite sure what her plan is. Belle walks over to the jackal with no fear, but I can feel the rest of us tensing up. All it would take is just one bite to fatally wound her, but Belle knows she's in charge. She leans down and gets in close to the Secondary's muzzle.

"Do you see how easy it would be for the Loch Ness Monster to kill you? To swallow you whole in one bite? But I'm not going to let him do that because you're a person and your life has value—*every life has value*. Do you understand what I'm saying? Everyone behind me has just as much value as you, regardless of where they fall in your stupid shifter hierarchy."

At this, the jackal cocks his head. I'm sure it's a novel idea for him. He's probably taken for granted the fact that he's higher up than most. He might not be a Tersh, but he's definitely not a lowly Primary. In his head, this makes him better.

"All right, here's the plan," Belle continues. "Grandpa Nessie, you keep jackal jerk here as collateral. The rest of us will go to the Isle of Man and check it out. If it isn't as the Secondary says—you can eat him. Well, maybe not all of him... just pieces. I don't think we should kill him outright, but if you eat his tongue and hands, he can't tell anyone anything."

The jackal looks ready to pass out at her words and promptly shifts back into human form.

"I swear I'm not lying!" he pants. "The dean's headquarters are at the Isle of Man!"

Belle waves a hand.

"Good, good. I'm glad you're not lying, but this is just our insurance."

"How will we get there?" Theo wonders.

Nestor raises an eyebrow at him. The disdain on his face is obvious. Clearly, he's still pissed that Belle slept with Theo and not him.

"We swim, obviously."

"I don't think I can swim to the Isle of Man," Belle interjects. "I'm pretty damn sure it's too far away."

"I was talking to the slippery dick here—*he* can swim."

Theo swallows thickly.

"I've never swam in the ocean," he admits.

"You'll be fine because you'll be with me," the niseag claims.

"Oh, delightful—and what about me?" Belle prods.

"You'll be riding me, lass," Nestor says with a waggle of his eyebrows.

"Listen, *pal*, I know you want to screw me, but—"

Nestor holds a hand up in vexation.

"I didn't mean *that* way—I meant 'ride me' like on my back while I swim."

Belle blanches.

"You want me to ride the Loch Ness Monster all the way to the Isle of Man?! That sounds dangerous."

I nod in agreement.

"She's right. It's a good way for you both to be spotted."

The Tersh just flaps his hand indifferently.

"Not if we go now," he negates. "It'll be too dark for anyone to see us, and I'm an exceptionally fast swimmer. It's just a matter of if the slippery dick here can keep up."

The double meaning isn't lost on Theo, who glares back at the smartarse Tertiary.

"I don't think it's *me* that has to keep up with *you*, but the other way around," he taunts boldly, and I'm surprised at his gall.

Belle laughs in delight, though, and kisses Theo's cheek.

"You're right—Nestor has to keep up with you now. But what about everyone else? How will they get to the island?" she wonders, bringing us back to topic.

Elise and Sian look at Jude who says they'll fly, but will need to take breaks.

"It'll be faster for us to fly there directly as opposed to going along the shoreline, but we'll still need to stop occasionally," he adds.

"And the others?" Belle prompts.

"They can ride us again," Jack offers.

I don't really like the idea, but being a horny toad means that I can only go so far on foot before tiring out, but arses can travel long distances and at faster speeds. We won't get there at the same time as the others, but at least we'll get there.

"I'm coming, too," my dad declares.

"As am I," my uncle echos.

"And me," my cousin tacks on.

Jack nods.

"Phineas and Arthur, you two can ride me. Dageus and Alastair, you two can ride Harry."

"What about us?" one of my clan's Elders inquires.

My uncle shakes his head.

"It's too dangerous. You must stay here and keep the clan together while we are away. You're in charge while I'm gone," Alastair decrees.

"Alastair!" another Elder roars. "He was in charge last time!

"No! It was Graham," the other refutes.

"No, it was you! Something bloody stupid happened I remember; so, *I* should be in charge."

"Neither of you ejits should be in charge—it should be me!" the last Elder proposes.

The three men begin to bicker amongst one another who should be left in charge, and my uncle just rolls his eyes. Everyone starts talking at once, and I clap my hands for attention.

"Do you really think that we should all go?" I ask hesitantly.

I don't want to say it out rightly because I know it will get me into a world of trouble, but I don't think Belle, Elise, nor Sian should join us. It's not safe for them. Thankfully, Jude understands what I'm trying to convey and nods.

"Yes, maybe only some of us should go—myself, Nestor, Jack, and Harry."

I nod encouragingly at this new plan, but Belle's already shaking her head. I realize that she'll never go for this idea because we all need to be together—that's what she thinks is safest.

"No, we leave the Secondary here with older Nessie, and we all go *together*. There's safety in numbers."

I know she's right, but I hate the thought of her potentially being caught by the dean or the doctor who injected her with whatever the fuck he concocted. We have no idea what's waiting on that island for us.

If we're not careful, it could spell our doom.

Chapter 24
Belle

"Just get on my back and hold on tightly—I'm slippery when wet."

"That's what she said," I mutter sourly as Nestor jumps into the waters of the North Channel and shifts into his massive Tertiary form.

Alastair drove us to the shore, which was only fifty minutes away from his house. Once we got there, Nestor immediately jumped out to get in the water, along with Theo. Elise, Sian, and Jude shifted and started flying south toward the Isle of Man seconds later. Harry and Jack are waiting in their ass forms for Phineas, Dageus, Arthur, and Alastair.

"You know... I might just ride Jack again," I say, hitching a thumb back at the land-roving group.

Nestor opens his big mouth and bellows at me, making me screech in fright.

"Ok, ok! I'm getting in!" I slowly ease into the water, terrified. "You know, you're not supposed to go to the ocean at night—there are sharks."

Nestor gives me a look to say, *'Do you think any sharks are around me?'*. To be fair, he *is* the baddest predator around. Theo looks even more hesitant than me, and I can't blame the guy. He doesn't even go into *lakes,* and now, he's just jumping right into the ocean. I smile encouragingly at him.

"Don't worry, we've got this," I lie, taking his hand and squeezing it.

He gives me a wan smile in return. My sweet slippery dick looks even paler in the moonlight with his blond hair nearly leached white and his big green eyes full of trepidation.

"Nestor won't let anything happen to you. Just remember what he said—*stay by his flipper*. You can ride it along with me. This way, we'll all stay together."

"I'm not a suckerfish," Theo murmurs. "It's going to be hard to keep up with your mate."

"*You're* my mate," I counter, "and you've got this. You can stay in the crook of my arm. Hopefully, I don't get hypothermia!"

"You'll be fine this time of the year," Theo reassures, and I pray to the shifter gods that he's right.

Nestor lets out another bellow, and I know it's time to shit or git. I wade into the water and swim the rest of the way. Climbing up onto Nestor's back, I decide to pretend he's just a dolphin—people pay hundreds of dollars to ride those things, and here I'm getting a free adventure on the back of the Loch Ness Monster.

Theo shifts and flips into the water. He comes back up and snuggles up close to Nestor's side. I scoop him up towards me, making sure he's still covered in water.

"Ok!" I holler back toward the shore at the others. "We'll see you there!"

At this, Nestor takes off. It's a good thing it's night because it would be pretty damn easy to spot a giraffe-sized neck coming out of the water with a woman clinging to it. Then again, at the speed that Nestor is going, maybe not. The man wasn't kidding—he can book it in water!

When I was a kid, my parents and I took a vacation to the Bahamas. I convinced my mom to go jet skiing with me. The foolish woman agreed—*moreover, she let me drive*. I'll never forget her screams of panic as I took us further and further away from the shore.

Riding Nestor is like riding a jet ski. A spray of ocean water slaps me in the face, cold, astringent, and pungent. It stings my eyes, but makes me feel alive. When I went jet skiing with my mom, we saw dark formations—shadows under the water—that I teased were for sure sharks. Smart woman that she is, my mom never let me jet ski again the rest of that vacation, but the experience always left me with a craving for exhilaration.

It's probably why I like to screw strangers so much—it gives me the same rush.

Riding Nestor's Loch Ness Monster is similar to banging a bunch of people you don't know at once. I wonder what kind of dark shadows lurk beneath the water, but they're nothing compared to the monster that's ferrying me across the Irish Sea. I check down at my arm every so often to make sure that Theo's still tucked in there. I can just barely see his scales glinting in the moonlight, but I know he's still there, safe and sound.

Nestor says we should arrive in approximately a few hours—I have no idea how far the Isle of Man is away from Scotland, but the shifter is like an aquatic mach jet! He keeps us close enough to the shore so that I can see it off to my left, but far enough away so that no one can spot us. At one point, Nestor takes us to the shore for a quick break. He shifts into his human form, as does Theo.

"What's up?" I wonder.

"Waterguard's coming by," Nestor answers. "We'll just lurk here for a moment."

I never see anything, but with my heightened senses, I can hear a boat off in the distance. It eventually passes, and we set off again. The Waterguard Incident makes me wonder how we're going to get close to the Isle of Man without any of the Tershes hearing us...

Maybe they'll be too inland?

Of course, that would have been too easy, right? When Nestor swims up to the island's shore, there is a pack of the most hideous looking animals I've ever seen waiting. Nestor shifts as he wades to land, cradling me—and fish Theo—in his arms. I feel so safe and protected.

That is, until the bastard tosses me onto my ass into the sand below.

The ugly fuckers in front of me growl menacingly at me before shifting into their human forms. They bow down to Nestor, who's holding Theo by his tail. The Loch Ness Dick-head drops my sweet mate onto the bank, where poor Theo flops before shifting and gasping in pain. I turn back to Nestor, ready to unleash my motherfucking fury, but he just raises a hand and gives me a feral smile.

"Go get your boss," he tells the shifters behind me. "Tell him I've brought a gift."

I stare at the traitor in shock; Theo's face mirrors my own. We didn't need to be quiet when we arrived to the island because this was Nestor's plan all along! I scowl darkly at the assclown as the other shifters subdue Theo and me. Struggle is futile—these jerks are ridiculously strong! Son of bitch, I should have castrated Nestor when I had the chance—but the fucker better watch his back.

I'm out for his dick now.

Chapter 25

Sian
THE TITMOUSE

I'm the fastest flier out of the three of us—Jude can go pretty far for an insect, but he tires out quickly and Elise's weight prevents her from keeping up with me—but my speed is no match for Nestor when he's in the water. We don't fly along the shore as the Tersh does, though, instead cutting straight across land.

After a few breaks, we reach the point where we need to cross the Irish Sea to the island. I don't particularly like crossing large bodies of water; I prefer to keep land in sight at all times. When I know we're nearing the island, I zip back to the others. Nestor really didn't explain to us what we should do when we get there, and I wish he had given us a more solid plan.

But because he's a Tertiary, we all just jumped into action.

I want to smack myself. We literally could just be flying into danger, and from the way that Jude's chittering, I know he's thinking the same thing. It would be wisest to fly back where Jack and Harry are taking the others and formulate a plan, but I really don't want to leave Belle alone that long. I lost track of her and Theo a long time ago and hope they're safe. Even though Belle's with Theo, I don't particularly trust Nestor—not after the high-handed way he made Belle his mate.

I swoop back to Elise and chirp at her. Although we're not the same species, I know she'll be able to understand the anxiety in my tweet—just as she is English and I am Welsh, occasionally our dialects differ, but ultimately, we get on fine. It's the same with our birds. I'm worried because, at this point, we have to land on the island. None of us have the stamina to make it back to the mainland to formulate a plan of attack. Elise sends me a soothing chirp in response, telling me it's ok. I twitter back quickly and do a loop around her before zipping ahead. She squawks at me to wait up, but I think it's best if I go and see if there's any danger.

I'd rather only I get hurt than her or Jude.

Flying as high as I can while still keeping to the side of the island, I scope the terrain below. The Isle of Man is many kilometers wide, and even though my bird site is keen, the higher I go, the less I can see. If I want to find Belle or Theo, I'm going to have to fly lower. Gradually, I descend cautiously and do a parameter check.

When I finish my circuit, I meet up with Elise and Jude. My six-legged shifter friend is tiring and will have to land soon. I chirp at the two of them, hoping that Jude understands that I think it's safe—well, as safe as it's going to be. I scent the air one more time just before Jude starts buzzing in agitation. It's then that I smell it—*a predator.* I swivel around quickly, but it's too late. A piercing screech fills the night air, and my small bird body quivers in fear.

Barreling down on us with lightning speed is a bird of prey.

Elise

THE BOOBY

I dart forward in the nick of time, knocking Sian out of the way, as the raptor comes bearing down on us. He clips my wing, and I start free falling from the sky. Before I know it, I smack into the water—hard. The pain is excruciating and takes my breath away. I unconsciously, instantly shift back into my human form. I can feel myself sinking into the deep, dark waters of the Irish Sea. It takes me a few seconds to shake off my stupor, and I realize I'm drowning. With panicked haste, I start swimming towards the surface. It's then I realize that the raptor broke my wing—which equals a broken arm.

Which equals being nearly helpless.

Trying to swim as best as I can with my left arm, my right one just dangles next to me, a useless dud. I kick powerfully with my legs, and by some miracle, I finally make my way to the surface and explode out of the water. Greedily, I gasp in more air, choking, coughing, and sputtering out droplets of water, trying to project them from my lungs. A splash sounds next to me, and a familiar head pops out.

It's Jude.

He swims over to me and wraps a hand around my waist before taking us to the shore.

"Thank you," I breathe, barely keeping my tears at bay. "Where's Sian?"

Jude doesn't answer, but just keeps doggedly swimming forward. When we finally drag ourselves wet, naked, and exhausted to the sandy banks, three wolverines meet us. They're the UK's most endangered animal—well, next to Nestor. The wolverines are nearly extinct and only live on the Isle of Man. They are vicious Tertiaries. A single one has more strength than a gorilla.— this translates into their human form as well, making them doubly dangerous. The three before us growl menacingly, I wonder if we would be safer in the water. But with my arm, it's certain that I'd drown. Not to mention this place is made for Tertiaries. I don't even want to think about what was probably lurking in those waters...

"Sian!" I cry. "Where is Sian?!"

My answer is just more growls. I wonder if Nestor, Theo, or Belle even made it. Jude looks positively apoplectic, and I know what he's thinking—we went into this blindly, foolishly. We listened to somebody because of our hierarchy, and it's probably led us to our own death. The three Tershes bare their teeth and swipe at us, showing nonverbally where they want Jude and me to go. It looks like we're being taken prisoner.

My only hope is that Sian managed to escape.

Chapter 26

Jude

THE COCKCHAFER

'm a fool a thousand times over.

I deserve to die for my stupidity, but not the others—not the ones I love. I really don't know what I was thinking when I just agreed to charge the Isle of Man with *no plan*. Nestor might have the manpower as the Loch Ness Monster, but I'm just a measly cockchafer. Even if the wolverines weren't shifters, it was foolish to just come upon their turf without a strategy. They're vicious creatures who can easily tear a person apart with one swipe as was the raptor who attacked Elise and me.

Of course, a Tertiary base where they're breeding humans and making an army to use against the world would be well guarded...

I don't know why I thought otherwise. The amount of air, land, and water Tershes surrounding us makes my skin crawl—*because I never sensed them*. Still, the wolverines haven't attacked us; whoever's in charge doesn't want us eaten just yet.

For now.

Hopefully, Nestor sensed the danger and got Belle and Theo out of here in time. As for Sian, I'm deeply worried. She flew back to the mainland with the raptor chasing her, but whether she can outmaneuver the bird of prey is the question—*she certainly can't outfly it.*

The wolverines snarl in unison, herding us inward on the island. I keep Elise close to me with a hand wrapped around her waist in support; I know her right arm is broken —the raptor did that. The height in which she dropped into the ocean makes my stomach twist. She's lucky that she didn't knock herself unconscious and drown. That's why I instantly flew down and shifted because I knew she had been injured. I feel like I have enough blood on my hands for the situation we're in. I won't have more of it. I won't lose anyone to my own stupidity.

We walk for about thirty minutes with me catching Elise as she stumbles to keep up. The branches are becoming thicker as we go deeper into the island. Where we're at isn't inhabited by anyone—it must be the protected grounds for the wolverines.

Great.

This is the *perfect* place for the Tershes to have head-quarters since nobody can disrupt the area and humans can't be on it.

Finally, we come to a stump where the three wolverines shift in unison—they're triplets. Elise and I stare in shock at the trio before our eyes. One walks over to the stump and kicks it with brute force. It rips out of the ground to reveal a grate that another one turns and opens before growling and pointing. I wonder if these Tershes even speak English or spend most of their time in their animal forms.

It's dark where we're at, and the trees around us shroud

the moonlight. Luckily, my shifter senses allow me to see better than most humans would be able to. Beneath the grate, is a gaping hole—and a tunnel that leads deep into the ground. The third wolverine shifter pushes Elise and me forward none too gently, indicating toward the dark hole where we're supposed to go.

"No fucking way!" Elise snaps.

In answer, the first wolverine kicks her behind the knee. She goes down with a howl of pain, and it takes everything in my strength to keep her upright. The movement nearly buckles my own knees with the strength that she was kicked with. My blood boils and rage sizzles along my nerve endings, but somehow I manage to keep it tamped down. I am no match for these men, and I won't put us at any more risk.

"I'll go down first," I whisper to Elise.

She looks at me with so much sorrow in her eyes, but she knows that we have no choice. I give her one last hug before climbing into the hole. Rung after rung, I go down, making sure that my steps are slow and steady. Occasionally, I touch Elise's leg to check if she's alright with her broken arm—I don't want her to slip and fall.

Further and further down we go, and I have no idea how deep this hellhole is. My cockchafer senses tingle when we finally reach the bottom—we're easily a quarter kilometer down. Being this far below sea level is very unsettling. I reach up to catch Elise as she reaches the bottom rung and set her down next to me.

Nudity isn't an issue for shifters, but I don't like the way the wolverines are looking at her like a piece of meat they can't wait to devour. They are the epitome of a true Tertiary —they think they can have whatever they want, whenever they want, because of what and who they are. The wolverines are above common decency and what they consider 'human rules'—and rape is a human rule. I hug Elise tenderly, knowing that she's scared not only for ourselves, but for Belle, Theo, and Sian. We must play our cards carefully if we want to come out of this alive, but I will happily sacrifice myself fighting these monsters if they harm Elise in any way.

We're led down a dark, sterile hallway. Even though all of my senses are heightened, I still can't hear anything—it's almost like sensory deprivation. It's unnerving, and I don't enjoy the sensation. Even more so, I despise not knowing what we're walking into, or where the wolverines are leading us.

I don't know how to prepare.

I don't know how to plan.

These Tertiaries have effectively manipulated my weakness without even knowing what it was—my need to be in control. After what seems like an eternity, we're led down another corridor and then into a room. This one has the lights on. As my eyes adjust to the brightness, they zero in on a corner where there are cages, and there inside kept like an animal, is Theo.

Belle is nowhere in sight.

Chapter 27
Belle

While Nestor's hailed as the cock of the walk, Theo and I are led to some underground bunker of hell in the middle of nowhere by a bunch of rabid men who look nothing like Hugh Jackman. I remember what Arthur said about my anger controlling my animal. I call upon it now, my rage a feral beast. But of course, I don't shift—which sucks because my ass snake would bite the shit out of these dill holes and kill them in a second.

Where's my black mamba when I need it?

The fickle fucker—that thing and I seriously need to have a talk. At a certain point, Theo and I are separated. I whimper, and Theo tries to run back towards me only to be sucker punched in the face, knocked out cold by one of the wolverines. I've never wanted to commit murder before or become a cannibal, but I'm pretty sure that I'm going to bite off Nestor's dick, eat it, and then slit his throat.

When I'm in Chimera form, of course.

I lick my lips, warming up to the idea. Maybe I'll gut him

with my claws or use my goat horn to stab him in the chest. My black mamba's just going to sit this one out.

A venomous death by a lethal toxin is too merciful and quick for that bastard.

"You better not hurt a hair on his head!" I snarl when one of the wolverines carelessly picks up Theo to sling him over his back and carry him off in the opposite direction.

Nestor follows them and I'm led away by the other two X-men fucks. No one acknowledges my threat, and so, I just keep ranting loudly as I walk down the hall. Finally, the wolverine shifter comes to a stop before a door that he opens. The sight that awaits me inside makes me screech in horror. There are five women tied to five separate beds—all in various states of pregnancy.

And if I'm not mistaken, one is giving birth.

"Stay," the wolverine man grunts.

It's the only word I've heard him use. He shuts the door behind me. I rush to it, but of course, it's locked. I turn back to the five women. Three look so frightened they might pass out, another looks ill, and the last one looks like a cross between excruciatingly pained and pissed—*which I can't blame her because it looks like she's ready to pop out a monster.*

"Are you the doctor?" she manages to grit out. "They said they were bringing me a doctor. I've been in labor for four hours, tied to this bed with no one!"

My stomach drops out my ass.

They weren't bringing anyone to help her, were they?

Which leads me to the inevitable conclusion that *I'm* going to have to help her. Inwardly, I'm having an absolute shitfit—a meltdown of epic proportions—but on the outside, I'm cool as a cucumber-cock. I slap a smile on my face and walk over to the sink to wash my hands.

"So, I'm Dr. Honey, and you have *nothing* to worry about. I've got you covered," I lie over my shoulder.

The other woman who looks terribly ill whimpers, as if she knows this. As long as nobody asks me for my credentials, we should be ship-shape, right?

"Ok," I croon soothingly, walking back over to the laboring woman with my freshly washed hands, "first things first—we need to get you more comfortable."

I stare at the woman who's tied to the bed, her hands pinned to her sides and her ankles spread open wide... this is going to be *a lot* harder than I thought. Looking around the makeshift hospital room, I search the cabinets under the sink until I find some tools—*if you would call them that.* I pull out one that I'm pretty for sure are forceps used to yeet a baby forcibly out of the womb—nothing says, 'welcome to the world' like being yanked into it. The sight makes me want to vomit, but I'm hoping the forceps are strong enough to help break the chains that are holding the woman down.

I walk back over to the woman and cheerfully explain that being tied down is *no* way to give birth. I clamp the forceps around one of the steel chains and pull as hard as I can... and end up breaking the fuckers—which is probably a good thing because *no* baby should have *forceps* used on them. Rage blinds me at the idea, and I can feel prickling under my skin. I quickly tamp it down because now is *not* the time to shift—but the sensation does give me a stroke of inspiration. Grabbing onto the chains, I rip with all my might, and to my surprise, they pull apart easier than my thighs after a dry sex spell. I make quick work of the other three chains before tossing them across the room and fist pumping the air.

"There can be only one Highlander!" I roar, feeling triumphant. "Braveheart's got *nothing* on me!"

Four of the women stare openly at me in shock, and the laboring woman looks deeply perturbed.

"Don't worry—that's *not* how I'm going to get your baby out," I hastily explain.

She doesn't look convinced in the least, and I realize I probably need to step up my bedside manner.

"Erm... have you worked on your breathing? You know, your hee-hee-hoos?" The woman's eyes widen, and she shakes her head. "Well, that's the first step," I coach. "I mean, at least that's what they say in Lamaze classes, don't they? I don't know. I'm not a—I mean, *of course, I know*. I'm totally a doctor—do you know how many times I've given someone a check-up? Well, more like a 'check out', but let's not get hung up on semantics. Not to mention, I've been elbow-deep in god-knows how many vaginas. I've got this thing in the bag. Alrighty, everyone, let's breathe together— on three. One, two, three. Hee-hee-hoo. Hee-hee-hoo."

All five women breathe with me like we're having a birth seance, and I swear that we're calling down the fertility gods. When I tell the woman to spread her legs wider and take a quick peek under the hood, I almost tap out. It's seriously enough to scare me celibate. This chick's wizard's sleeve is stretched to epic proportions—*and something is crowning.*

Motherfucking crowning.

I suddenly understand how Will Smith felt in the movie *Men in Black* when Reggie's wife is giving birth to that squid thing.

"Something's peekin'!" I quote out loud in absolute horror. Instead of a squid tentacle popping out, it looks like a furry muzzle trimmed with teeth. "Oh, my god, her vagina has teeth."

"What do you mean it has teeth?!" the laboring woman screeches, and I realize I accidentally spoke out loud.

"Did I say teeth?" I fake laugh. "I meant fangs."
At this, the woman promptly passes out.
Whelp, shit sticks.
I'm doing this mission on my own, aren't I?
This lady better name her kid after me.

Chapter 28
Belle

"*Hee-hee-hoo. Hee-hee-hoo.*"

Even though the woman's unconscious, I still do the breathing because, honestly, I don't want to pass out. Then who's going to give birth? I watch as the thing protruding from the woman's vagina tries to squeeze itself out.

That's impressive.

It's starting to look like a face that's been stretched against cellophane. Yep, I'm definitely going to need therapy after this. After a moment, it doesn't look like it can go any further; so, I decide to help it. And would you believe it— the little fucker nips at me! Thank goodness it's got a vagina around it so it can't open its jaws all the way to take a real bite. I smack it, making the thing yelp, but keep trying to help it out.

So much therapy.

I'm elbow deep in birth sauce when suddenly the door slams open. I barely spare the person a glance because I'm too focused on my task.

I hear the person mumble, "What the fuck is going on in here?"

It's Nestor.

The bastard is lucky that I'm otherwise occupied at the moment.

"Why the fuck are these women chained to the bed? Is that one in labor? Why are her chains ripped off? Did she do that?!"

"No," I respond coolly. "I did—can you just imagine what I'm going to do to your dick?"

Nestor raises both hands.

"Easy, love, I swear I'm not with the wolverines and other Tershes. I was just doing it to distract them."

I can't tell if it's the truth I hear ringing in his words or just my desperation that he's on our side because I *really* need some help.

"Listen, pal, you can explain and apologize *later*. Right now, we've got a situation on our hands. We need to help this woman give birth."

Nestor looks over my shoulder.

"Is she even awake?!"

"No!" I screech. "That's why we've got to do this *now*!"

The Loch Ness Fuckup leans down to take a gander between the lady's legs and stands back up so quickly, he almost bowls me over.

"Wh-wh-what is *that*?" Nestor stammers.

Nothing unnerves a man quicker than a woman giving birth to an unknown creature.

"It's a surprise!" I shout snarkily. "Now, push down on her stomach!"

Nestor's face turns the same color as his monster's skin.

"Don't you even think about passing out!" I roar.

Seriously, how many unconscious people am I going to have to deal with today?

The pretend traitor finally makes his way over to the woman and gently rests his hands on her stomach.

"I can't push," he cringes.

Any other time, I would be touched by the care and reverence he's showing to this pregnant chick...

Unfortunately, today is *not* that day.

"PUSH!" I scream.

Nestor's hands act of their own accord, and he slams down to project the... *whatever* out. The thing comes barreling out of the woman's vaginat, into my arms, and knocks me flat on my ass.

Well, this whole experience totally gives new meaning to the word 'birth cannon'.

Staring down at the sticky creature, I realize what I thought was a muzzle is actually a beak attached to what seems to be maybe a lion—but with wings.

How come this lion-thing gets wings?!

Because this isn't a creature like me. It's not a chimera.

No—it's a motherfucking griffin!

It would seem like Dr. Fuckface's genetic splicing is yet another success.

"Oooo—we can name him Gryffon!"

"We're naming the griffin 'griffin'? Seems unoriginal, lass." Nestor comments.

"It's brilliant! Besides, we can argue later. We need to get these women out of here."

"Right—and get Theo, Jude, and Elise."

"Jude and Elise?!" I screech.

"Ow, lass! Lower the volume of your voice. My ears are bleeding."

I give him a sour look.

"Why are Jude and Elise here?!"

"Ask *them*, lass. In the meantime, I've got the women. You carry *Gryffon*. Follow me."

In a fantastical feat of strength that makes the wolverines look like whiny little bitches, Nestor somehow manages to carry *all* five women in his arms. I can see his shoulders strain as he strives to make sure they're all comfortable.

Between us, I fall a little in love with him.

Nestor dashes out of the room, and I sprint to keep up with the baby in my arms. He looks like a griffin, but I swear he's a heifer. The Loch Ness Tersh leads me to another room that has cages.

Cages.

And inside are my friends.

Yep—I'm definitely becoming a murderer.

Sorry, mom.

Using my own strength, I rip off the lock holding the cage shut. Jude, Theo, and Elise stare at me in shock. I wink at them. If this doesn't get their engines revving, I don't know what will.

"This way!" Nestor shouts, and I remember he's holding five women—one who's bleeding profusely—in his arms.

I chase after him with Gryffon in my arms and the others following me. We weave this way and that in what seems like an underground labyrinth before Nestor brings us to an elevator.

AN ELEVATOR!

Peeps are dying—slowly and excruciatingly.

The elevator takes us topside and opens in a fancy looking office that has me asking so many questions.

"Not now, love," Jude whispers.

"Thanks for belting her up," Nestor whispers back, and I glare at him.

We race out of the building and back toward the Irish Sea. It's dark, but our senses guide us well enough. Eventually, the lapping of water on the shore greets our ears, and I know we're close. Seconds later, the sea comes into view.

"Look—over there!" Elise exclaims. "A boat!"

We run down and all clamber on board after Nestor checks it first. I really hope somebody can drive this bitch. Of course, Jude knows exactly what he's doing—I'm going to bang him so good when we're out of this mess. He turns the thing on, revs it up, and we get the hell out of there.

"Yeah!" I shout into the night. "Let's blow this popsicle stand—the Isle of Dicks sucks!"

We're not very far into the Irish Sea when I see the all too familiar danger sign of a *fin* popping out of the water—and not just one.

Hundreds.

Holy shit, are they filming Shark Week?!

I can star in my own *Jaws* movie—all I'm missing is the theme music to my own death.

The aquatic carnivores start circling us in calculated ways that tell me they're not normal sharks. *They're shifters.*

Huh... I wonder if they're like Maui from *Moana* and become half-man, half-shark—only the top half is the shark.

Then I remember Arthur saying that splicing is painful and shifters rarely survive it.

Please turn Maui.

Please turn Maui.

"Is she chanting to the Hawaiian God of Trickery?" Elise demands to Jude, but I don't bother responding.

I'm so sick of being scared of being eaten or violated by another human—I mean, shifter—either way, it's fucked up!

Suddenly, something eight times the size of the boat and

easily fifteen times bigger than the sharks comes bursting out of the water, knocking three sharks at least fifty feet into the air!

"Ah! Take cover!" I cry, throwing my hands over my head —*because that's definitely going to protect me from shark missiles.*

Watching the now flying aquatic carnivores, I'm terrified that they're going to land inside the boat and capsize us, but a long neck comes out and catches all three sharks at once, biting them in half, and swallowing them whole. I realize it's Nestor. With sudden clarity, I realize exactly why Arthur's uncle didn't fight Nestor when he said he wanted me as his mate—this is one badass Tertiary!

"Go, Nessie! Eat all them shark bitches!" I cheer.

The others yell with me—even the pregnant women, and I'm glad to see their smiles.

All of a sudden, Nestor turns quickly, smacking the boat with his big ass flipper. I go sailing to the side where the bar slams into my solar plexus, effectively knocking the air right out of me. I lose my balance and topple head first into the Irish Sea.

Dear, sweet Jesus, please let Nestor have eaten all the sharks first is my last thought as I go under.

Chapter 29

Theo

THE SLIPPERY DICK

"*D*rive the boat, get to the mainland, find the others."

With this command, Jude just jumps into the water where Belle went under. The barmy man—doesn't he know that Nestor will protect her? Of course, there's no guarantee Nestor will get to her in time, and with everything at stake—Elise and her broken arm and five pregnant women—I need to get to the mainland immediately. I've never wanted a hospital so desperately. Whipping the boat around, I punch the acceleration and do as I have been bid. Elise comes up to me, her arm still dangling helplessly at her side, and I can only imagine the amount of pain she's in.

"Theo, we've got to hurry," she whispers.

"What's wrong?"

"It's the woman who gave birth to Gryffon. She's losing blood rapidly. If we don't get her to the hospital for a transfusion soon, she's going to die."

My heart accelerates at these words. I want to wait for

Belle, Jude, and Nestor, but time is of the essence. I've got to trust them to take care of themselves—just as Jude has entrusted me with the care of Elise, these women, and the baby. I know that Arthur and the others are waiting for us, but we still don't know where Sian is.

It feels as if my entire life has been pulled apart, and all I can do now is salvage the broken pieces left behind.

I wish Jude hadn't jumped into the water. And I guess if I'm being honest with myself, I wish it had been me—I wanted to be the hero for once.

The one to save my mate.

But getting this boat to the mainland is just as heroic; there are other lives to save here.

Hopefully, I can maneuver the thing and not crash it. I drive straight east. Eventually, I'll have to hit the shore. Gryffon whines in Elise's arms and nips at the air.

"Do you think he's hungry?" she wonders.

The little marvel still hasn't shifted into his human form.

"How are we going to feed him when he's like this?" I counter. "Especially when his mum is sick."

"She wouldn't feed him anyway," Elise sniffles. "She hates the poor mite. She considers him an abomination—considers *us* abominations!"

Her words break my heart.

This poor human woman will never realize that her sweet baby is perfectly normal and not a monster. I quirk a smile at his name. Of course, Belle would want to name the griffin 'Gryffon'. The baby makes me think of my mate, and I hope that she's ok. But I know Jude and Nestor won't let anything happen to her. In return, I'll do my damned best to make sure nothing happens to these women. Belle did what most people probably wouldn't have—she saved Gryffon's life as well as the other women's lives by ensuring they joined us. She wasn't leaving anyone behind. I won't have her sacrifice be in vain.

I don't have the lights for the boat turned on because I don't want to alert any Watergaurds, but it's still dark out. Soon it will be dawn, but the moon does nothing to show me my way. I've often traversed from North Ireland to the mainland UK by ferry. It never took more than forty minutes, but I've never done this from the Isle of Man. I live in constant fear that I'll misjudge the distance and ship-wreck us all. Even still, I push the boat to go faster while remaining cautious. The water's placid at the moment, but our speed is causing it to become choppy. I waffle between getting to the mainland quickly or slowing down for a smoother ride. I don't want to cause any more pain for the pregnant women or Elise.

Minutes go by, and eventually, I hear the tweet of a bird. I sigh in relief—that sound is always a good sign. Birds mean land. *Just as long as it's not a predator.* But the sound is too sweet and high-pitched. It gets closer and closer, and I see a familiar bird circling the boat. She swoops down and shifts into Sian. Elise nearly drops the baby griffin in her joy.

"Where did you get *him* from?!" the Welsh shifter demands.

"It's a *long* story," Elise chuckles. "Can you take him, though? My arm really hurts."

Sian takes the baby shifter from Elise, staring at him curiously.

"What is he?"

"He's a griffin, and we've named him Gryffon—well, *Belle* named him Gryff," Elise explains, making Sian laugh.

"Of course, she did. He's a cute little guy."

Gryff opens his beak to squawk at Sian before promptly trying to bite her fingers.

"Is he hungry?"

"We think so," I comment, "but his mom wants nothing to do with him. Besides, she's not in any condition anyway. We need to get her to a hospital immediately—not to mention the four other women aboard as well as Elise."

Sian's eyes widen when she takes in the other women, understanding the magnitude of the situation and just what the Tershes have done.

"Oh god, this is a disaster," she breathes in horror.

I snort.

No—it's a fucking nightmare come to life.

Chapter 30

Belle

One second, I'm cheering on Nestor for eating the sharks; the next, *I'm swimming with them.*

The water is dark, cold, and salty. It's a hell of a lot different than riding on Nestor's back, I can tell you that. Anxiously, I try to make my way to the surface, but the thrashing around me keeps pulling me under. Nestor's creating a riptide with his movements. He doesn't realize I'm in the water, too. If he doesn't stop, I'm likely to drown.

I feel something tug at my foot, and foolishly, I scream, forgetting that I'm underwater. I get a mouthful of salty brine as my punishment. I clamp my lipa shut and push out my nostrils forcibly.

If I don't get air soon, my death certificate will read 'drowned to death'—and not because of too much cum.

The thing on my foot clamps down harder and tries to drag me away. Dammit, Nestor didn't get all the sharks, and now, one of them is surely going to eat me. I'm not even going to die of drowning. I really don't know what's worse or which death I would prefer—eaten by a shark or drowning *not in jizz*. If I *had* to choose, I would pick neither. Both are absolutely sucky options, and I want nothing to do with them... unless it changes to drowning on jizz.

The gods of emergency birth control must hear my prayers, though, because whatever is eating me is also pulling me toward the surface. *At least, I won't drown while being eaten.*

I once read that ants have a sour taste when they're afraid, making them less likely to be eaten by predators, and I wonder if that's what I'm like. Perhaps the shark wants to get me back to the surface so I'm a little less panicked and more flavorful.

Makes sense.

We burst out of the water, and I've never appreciated air as much as I do in this moment. I gulp it up greedily while coughing—it's hard to breathe when you're still choking on water—but I try. Every cavity in my sinuses burns like hell. I harness that anger and shift—but cats hate water.

Chimeras are no different.

Plus, the added weight of my billy goat really doesn't help. So, I shift back into human form and swivel around with my fist ready to punch the shark prepared to eat me.

Because everybody knows you punch a shark in the snout to get it to *not* eat you.

When I turn, I see that it's Jude! I throw both my arms around him, nearly sending us back under the water again.

"Jude, you beautiful man—I could kiss you!"

I can barely make out his features, even though he's only inches from my face. His hair is inky black and slicked back, but even I can see the smoldering fire in his dark eyes. Being the hussy that I am, I take it as an invitation. I pull him to me, and I kiss him with all the passion and pent-up lust that I feel for him. There's also gratitude that he saved me and awe for his ceaseless amount of knowledge, but mostly it's just good old sexual attraction because Jude is one fine piece of ass. He reminds me more of Jack—there's no shyness to him like with Arthur and Theo. There's an assertive dominance that I can get behind any day of the week. I pull back and lick the outer shell of his wet ear.

"The safety word is 'fuck me harder'."

Jude sputters out of a laugh.

"What?!"

"The safety word—it's 'fuck me harder'. And by safety word I just mean fuck me harder."

I wrap my naked form around his and line his dick up to my opening perfectly. I waggle my eyebrows as I slip down on a shaft.

"Now, I can cross off ocean boning from my fuckit list," I croon in satisfaction.

Jude chuckles, but attempts to push me off of him.

"Now is not the time."

Suddenly, a head pops up next to us.

"What the hell's going on here?!"

It's Nestor, and he's in human form again.

"Ocean boning!" I crow.

"Oooo, let me in on that action."

Jude huffs in vexation.

"What about the others?"

"I saw the boat take off toward the mainland," Nestor comments.

"Yes, I told Theo to head in that direction because we desperately need to get those women to a hospital."

"No worries. I can get us to the mainland, too. Right after

we all ocean fuck," Nestor stipulates. In the dim light, I watch Jude blanch.

"We are *not* fucking!" he snaps at Nestor.

"Not you and I! I meant my mate and I. She's already on you. Let her ride you while I watch. It turns me on. Then, it'll be my turn, and I'll show you how a *real* man fucks."

Jude gives him an absolutely sour look and scoffs, "I think I can do just fine on my own, thank you."

"Prove it," Nestor challenges smugly.

"Yeah," I taunt Jude. "*Prove it.*"

He stares back at me with a look that says, 'challenge accepted'. Jude's natural assertiveness comes to the forefront as he wraps my legs tighter around his waist.

"Hold on," he murmurs in my ear before jackhammering into me back and forth.

The man's ability to keep us above the water while giving me one of the most delicious dickings in my life is truly glorious. I hope Nestor is taking notes. Being in the water makes you practically weightless, and Jude effortlessly pulls me up and down. The motion is fluid and graceful—just like him. Within seconds, he has me coming, and I'm glad that Nestor took care of all the water predators because they could surely smell my feminine slickety-frickety.

Being the consummate British gentleman, Jude makes me come *five* more times before he finds his own release. I don't want to say anything, but Nestor has some seriously *stiff* competition. I grin at my mental sex pun as Jude fills me with sperm floaties. Nestor shoves him away, ripping me from Jude's warm body.

"My turn," he growls in his thick brogue.

He slams right into me from behind—a novel position I never thought to do in water. Of course, I'm wet and ready, but Nestor doesn't seem to care. He knows that I like it rough. One of his hands splays across my stomach, keeping me pinned to him as he thrusts into me from behind. His other hand is wrapped around my throat, two fingers hooked into my mouth. He's rubbing them seductively back and forth, and I lean forward to bite the salty tips.

"Ah, a nipper, are we, lass. Two can play at that," he whispers before biting down where my shoulder meets my neck.

The unexpected move has me coming faster than anything.

Nestor laughs triumphantly and yells tauntingly at Jude, "That, my boy, is how it's done!"

Jude just raises a brow while treading water—*how are these men not exhausted?*

I'm not, but only because they've been holding me up.

"You still have four more to go," Jude reminds Nestor of their little sexual competition.

I can feel Nestor grin at my neck or into my hair. He doesn't stop at four—or five, or six, *or seven*. By the eighth orgasm, I'm begging *him* to stop. Only then does he finally find his own release. He gently pulls out of me—a sweet contrast to the roughness in which we fucked—before handing me to Jude to shift into his Loch Ness Monster.

Jude helps me clamber onto his back, which is slippery and my legs are like jelly. Once I'm seated, Jude pulls himself up behind me, and Nestor takes off like a bolt of lightning. As the sea water splashes into my face, everything comes crashing down around me when I remember the situation.

Effectively breaking my post-orgasm bubble.

"Dammit! We didn't get to spork!" I complain.

"What's sporking?" Jude wonders.

"You know—spooning, but with a raging boner."

Jude laughs.

"Maybe Nestor and I can spork you at the same time," he suggests.

My clam quivers at the thought.

I guess I just crossed one thing off my fuckit list to add another.

Chapter 31

Jack

THE ASS

"We've got a situation, come on!"

No sooner than Sian utters these words, she shifts right back into a bird and flies off, expecting us all to follow. I look over at my cousin, Arthur, Dageus, Alastair, and Phineas.

"She must have found the others!" I shout. "Hurry—we can just walk there."

I don't feel like shifting again, or anyone riding me. We run to the shore to find a boat. On board, I spot Theo, Elise, and five women I've never seen. Elise's one arm is hanging at her side, and I immediately know it's broken.

When we first came to the shore to wait for the others, I saw how foolish our plan was—*because we didn't have any*. It only became worse when Sian came flying in *with a bird of prey chasing her*. I'll never forget the look of fright on her face as she shifted midair to land on the beach. She might have been terrified, but she was also mighty furious. She grabbed a stick of driftwood and smacked the bird chasing her as hard as possible—sent the damned thing skipping back out to the Irish Sea. The sweet bird has quite an arm. If there's any justice, she hurt the bastard badly enough so that it couldn't come back.

With her mission accomplished, Sian immediately collapsed with exhaustion. I gathered her into my arms where she explained what happened back on the Isle of Man. Without a shadow of a doubt, I knew I had to get there —*but how?* We had no means. Sian relaxed and rested until she could fly again. We knew it was risky--nobody wanted her to do it—but she was our only option. And being the stubborn, feisty bird that she is, Sian wouldn't take no for an answer. Over and over, she kept flying back and forth, doing her rounds. Obviously, this last time she finally had found something—except I have no idea who these pregnant women are nor where Belle, Jude, or Nestor are.

A whimpering cry catches my attention, and I see Elise handing Sian *a baby*. He seems rather large, and I'm not sure if he's a shifter or not. Degas, Alistair, Arthur, Harry, and I go over to help Theo with the women.

"Whose baby is that?" I ask him as I help one pregnant lady up.

She looks like she's bleeding heavily and needs a doctor immediately.

"It's *her* baby," Theo whispers, nodding down to the woman in my arms.

Even though she looks like death, she manages to snarl, "That's not my baby!"

I look back at the others with wide eyes. I've never heard such hatred spewed—especially towards an innocent babe! We get the women situated a little further inland where we have some cover of trees. There, Theo and Elise explain what happened. Turns out that the baby boy just changed into his human form and that he's a lot like Belle. Gryffon is what they call them, because, well, he's a griffin.

"What are we going to do" Phineas mutters in worry.

"I don't know," Alastair murmurs. "It's not looking good, though. We need to get these women to a hospital, but how are we going to get them there?"

"We can't go to a hospital... they're not giving birth to *human* children," Elise reminds.

A familiar bellow has my ears perking up.

"Nestor!" Arthur and I say at the same time.

"Everyone, stay here! We'll go check it out!"

Together, Arthur and I race back to the shore. Nestor's in his Loch Ness Monster form with Belle and Jude riding his back. She jumps off Nestor's back, and I splash into the water to hug her tightly to me. The Tersh shifts and both him and Jude place a protective hand on her shoulder. Unconsciously, both men are declaring her as their mate. I give a small bow to both, acknowledging their claim. As long as there's a place for Arthur, Theo, and myself, we'll be ok. Belle is asking a hundred questions per second.

"Yes, everyone got here safely. Yes, Elise is ok. No, no one else is giving birth. Yes, Gryff is fine. No, he's not an animal anymore. He's a human baby," I answer.

At this, Belle squeals.

"Take me to them!"

I scoop her up into my arms and dash the short distance back to everyone else. Phineas has kindly brought clothing for everyone, and I can see the relief on her face to finally be covered again.

"I thought you liked being starkers," I tease her.

"I never thought I'd say this—but I think I've had enough nudity for a lifetime," she jokes.

All of a sudden, Alastair cries out and Jude goes running

over to the woman who gave birth. She's gasping and convulsing uncontrollably. The two men try to ask her questions, but it's like she can't hear, and in seconds, she passes. All of us stare in shock—especially the four remaining women who are pregnant.

"Oh my god!" Belle sobs. "We need a doctor. We need a doctor *right now!*"

At this, Harry chimes, "Psst, paging Dr. Papa Roach. Psst, paging Dr. Papa Roach."

Normally I would smack him because now's *not* the time for levity—but he's right.

It's Jude's time to shine.

Chapter 32

Belle

"Jude—you're a doctor?!" I can feel my mouth gaping open in shock—but it's because I'm shocked! Jude doesn't even spare me a glance, immediately setting to work to help all of his patients.

And there's a lot of them.

He barks out a few commands to Jack, Harry, and Alastair before replying to me.

"Yes, I knew I was never going to get the respect of my kind; so, I decided to become one of the most prestigious professions there is in the human world. At least then maybe someone would think I'm useful."

My heart breaks at his words.

Softly, knowing that he can't hear me, I whisper, "You have nothing to prove."

I walk over to Sian, who is holding the squalling baby. He looks months old as opposed to just hours old. Once Jude sets Elise's arm and adds the makeshift splint from supplies on the boat, he turns to us.

"These women need to have C-sections or else they'll die, too."

I look around at a loss.

"This is no place for surgery! It's not sterile, and you don't have the proper tools. The women will surely die if you attempt anything!"

Jude nods sadly, clearly thinking the same thing, and I wonder if it would have been best if we had just left the women back at the facility. At least there—*no.* I shake my head at this thought. *Nothing* was better there—they were chained down like animals left to give birth on their own.

Probably to die.

"We need to get them to a hospital. It's the only way!" I say.

Alastair shakes his head. "We can't do that. Look at what they're giving birth to! The humans—"

"The humans will what?!" I shout. "Whether you like it or not, humans are being brought into this war. They're going to know what's happening eventually. Is it really worth losing any more lives? Is your secret really worth keeping at this point? Because the Tertiaries don't give a fuck! They're going to try to take over regardless. At least we can attempt to get the humans on our side, prepare them for the situation, and do what's better for all of us."

I can tell the man flat out hates the idea, but what other choices do we have? And I know that I'm right. Not all humans are monsters—and I highly doubt they can be any worse than what the Tershes are.

"Listen," Arthur interjects, "we're in Ravenglass. The closest hospital is only a quarter hour away. Why don't we call some shifter doctors that we know to meet us? We can come in, go through the E.R., and say that we're there for emergency procedures. At least then *maybe* we can take the babies out without anyone realizing what they are."

I give Arthur a look.

"It's a solid plan considering, but I don't know how hospitals are here in the UK, but in the states, they tag you with wristbands that you have to scan you to even hold your baby, let alone leave the hospital with it. If your wristband doesn't match up with the baby's, you're shit out of luck."

That's right... because in America, people walk into hospitals and steal babies.

#whatthefuck

Maybe it's not the way here in the UK, though. Maybe we can just stroll out of British hospital with four Shifter babies all easy-peasy-lemon-squeezy.

It's not like we really have many other options.

"Ok, but do we know any doctors around here that can get here in time?" I wonder.

One of the pregnant women lets out a low moan, and I'm pretty sure that she's in labor.

"You guys, we need to figure this out now—"

But the rest of my sentence is drowned out by a terrifying, ferocious roar.

"What was that?" one of the pregnant women quakes.

"The wind," I fib.

Everyone looks at me skeptically, and I shrug.

At least I tried.

Seconds later, something from my worst nightmare comes crashing out through the trees. It looks like a wolf —*but on roids*. It's easily five times larger than any wolf I've ever seen. Its eyes are glowing red, and I'm really beginning to think that Dean Stiffdick has no damn clue what he's talking about when it comes to real and not real animals.

"A dire wolf," Arthur breathes by me.

"What?" I blurt.

"They're one of the rarest wolves ever. A legend. A myth. Said to live in northern Siberia, and only seen by a handful of locals."

Of fucking course.

The gigantic beast snarls out another roar before giving me a very familiar wolfy grin—I realize *this* is Dean Stiffdick. From out of the mist behind him, I can just barely make out Dr. Fuckface in his human form walking towards us in the early dawn light.

"Give me the baby," he commands.

I hitch a thumb at the little guy sleeping in Sian's arms.

"You mean Gryffon?"

"Yes, the griffin"

"No, his *name* is Gryffon."

"No, he *is* a griffin."

"Yes, but we've *named* him Gryffon."

Dr. Fuckface looks confused.

"You named the griffin 'Griffin'?"

"Yeah, it makes sense, right?" I continue. "But call him Gryff for short. Super cute, huh? And instead of spelling it like griffin, we're going to spell it G-r-y-f-f-o-n."

Dr. Fuckface clamps a hand over his ears.

"Enough!" he roars. "I don't want to hear your stupid Yank muttering anymore!"

I cross my arms in affront.

"Rude!" I huff.

Why does everything have to be an American insult?

Like I ramble *because* I'm American. I know plenty of British people that ramble... I just can't name any right now.

"We're taking the baby."

This comes from the dire wolf, and I almost shit myself.

Dean Stiff Dick can talk when he's an animal. Correction—*this* is my worst nightmare.

"I'll also be taking all the pregnant women, too. Oh, and you, Belle."

At this, Nestor jumps before me.

"No, you're not! No one lays a finger on my mate!"

"Yeah—I'm like his Butterfinger Bitch!" I tack on.

The doctor steps forward, his hands spread wide in supplication.

"There's no need for us to be enemies," he murmurs to Nestor, completely ignoring me and my Yank ramblings. I snort.

"Um, yes, there *is* a need for us to be enemies because *you're* a dick who wants to fuck everyone over."

The fuckstick continues to pointedly ignore me, directing his attention only at Nestor.

"Our kind can come together and be superior as we were meant to be."

"Don't listen to him, Nestor," I whisper from the corner of my mouth. "It's a trap!"

"Would you shut the fuck up!" the doctor snaps, and I step around Nestor to get in his face.

It's then that I see in his hand the familiar glint of a syringe full of fuck-knows-what liquid. I screech and stumble back. My panic triggers Nestor, and he shifts to defend me—but a sea creature the size of Nessie shouldn't shift on land. He's immediately beached, and I'm concerned his lungs will compress and he'll die.

In the ensuing confusion, Dean Stiffdick takes advantage by grabbing my arm and bodily tossing me up onto his back before running off. He's going so fast that I'm scared if I fall, I'll break every bone in my body. I cling onto the monster for dear life. Before I know it, I'm back at the shore, being led aboard another boat to be spirited away to fuck knows where. A screeching caw sounds in the air as a giant bird drops down from the sky. It might be a hawk or condor —I don't know, I'm not an animal expert—and it shifts into Dr. Fuckface.

Ugh.

How dare he be something so badass.

The jerk deserves to be nothing more than a maggot.

Beside him, Dean Hardwick has shifted, too, and I realize I'm alone on a boat with two naked assholes who want to breed me.

This is just not my semester.

Chapter 33

Sian
THE TITMOUSE

I rock the sweet baby boy to sleep as Jude sets Elise's broken arm. She won't be able to shift any time soon—not at the detriment of rebreaking her wing. I watch an imperceptible wince of pain flash across her features before her face becomes placid and stoic once more. Elise is a lot like Jude—all her battles are kept hidden on the inside. It's easier for her to contain her feelings that way. My feelings are on my sleeve: messy, loud, and in your face—like the tears streaming down mine because I can't stand the pain the love of my life is in.

The whole situation turns my stomach. Watching that woman die for no reason, holding her newborn baby that she didn't want because she thought it was a monster, and seeing the four other women fear that their fate will be the same. I gaze down at the poor, sweet, innocent babe in my arms. Gryff never asked for any of this to happen to him. I place a gentle kiss on his soft brown curls.

"Little Gryffon, I love you," I whisper in his ear.

All babies need to know that they're loved unconditionally, no matter how they were brought into this world. Jude finishes with Elise, and she comes over to stand by me. I show her Gryff, asleep in my arms, knowing she wishes she could hold him. But until she's in a better location and seated, she can't. We simply can't afford to do any more damage to her arm, especially without any x-rays. But Jude is one of the top doctors in the central UK. He definitely knows what he's doing, and we're lucky to have him. Talk turns to the four pregnant women and what to do about them. My stomach rolls when it's decreed they need a C-section, or they'll die.

Our options are extremely limited.

Nobody says it out loud, but the chances of them surviving are slim to none anyways. Are they all pregnant with more griffins? Or are they different animal hybrids? The little guy asleep in my arms seems to have similar traits as the others of my species—he shifted into human form within hours of his birth.

But who's to say he can't shift back?

Who's to say anything?

We know nothing about what he is. All I know is we need to get him to safety. My thoughts are interrupted by the scent of something predatory on the wind. I smell him before I hear him—a Tertiary of epic proportions—but every time I've finally become attuned to a nearby Tersh, it's always been too late.

This time is no exception.

When a monstrous creature comes crashing through the brush, I know it can only be none other than the dean who did this to Belle. Moments later, a man in human form comes sauntering behind the shifted dean. I can tell that he is a shifter, as well. There's a familiarity about him that sets me on edge. When I sniff the air, I realize I recognize the scent—it's the bird of prey that chased me, that hurt Elise, and that I hit with the branch! Even this close, his scent is faint, making me wonder if he's masking it somehow. And of course, fate would decree that the bastard broke Elise's wing, but I hit him with a massive tree branch and he's perfectly dandy.

"Give me the baby," he demands.

I clutch Gryffon to me even tighter. Over my dead body is this monster taking my sweet baby from me. Elise edges closer to my side. Normally, she would stand in front of me. She's always been the more protective bird of our pairing, being so much taller than me, but with her broken arm, she's not nearly as strong as usual. Of course, it's Belle—our kind, brave Yank— who confronts the man. I don't know why I'm surprised since she has no idea of the laws in our world nor any true clue to who she's standing up against.

Or maybe she just doesn't care because that's the type of person she is.

She's always standing up for what's right, and right now, she's standing up against the biggest and the baddest wolf in all the land.

For us.

For Primaries.

Elise
THE BOOBY

One second, Belle is arguing with the shifter who broke my wing and the next, Nestor has shifted into his Tertiary form. He collapses to the ground and snaps out with his teeth, but the weight of animal form is crushing him.

Gravity's a bitch when you're a two thousand kilogram monster meant to live in water.

In his great pain, I don't know if Nestor can shift back into human form, but if he doesn't do it quickly, he'll die. His long tail comes thrashing out, and I shove Sian and the baby to the ground. We hit hard, and I hear Griffin crying. I pray that I haven't hurt him in any way. An ear-piercing scream rends the air, and I realize it's Belle. I quickly stand up in time to see the dire wolf take her in his mouth and run away with her.

The world around me is utter bedlam. Arthur and Jack are yelling at Nestor to shift back into his human form while Jude, Harry, Theo, Phineas, Dageus, and Alalstair are trying to calm down the pregnant women. Suddenly, a familiar shriek echoes in my ears, and I see the doctor fly off into the early morning light, leaving this shitshow behind him. As if things can't get any worse, the woman who had been moaning before now cries out in great pain, and I know she's about to give birth. The other three women start wailing in panic, and Gryff, still scared from what happened before, joins in. Tears are leaking from Sian's eyes, too, and I wish I could do something to soothe her.

Everything around us feels like total pandemonium, but by some miracle, Nestor finally shifts back into human form. He takes large gulps of air before passing out. Jack checks his pulse while Jude helps the woman in labor. He's gently coaching her on what to do when a sickening, ripping sound sounds around us. From between the woman's legs drops a creature larger than most overfed, household cats. It rolls over, and to my horror, I see it has three heads—all different breeds of dog.

Rottweiler, Doberman, and German Shepard.

I realize the mad scientist and the dean have created something from Greek fiction—their very own Cerberus. The woman who just gave birth collapses to the ground. Jude and I watch helplessly as she bleeds out. For the first time in my life, I despise my kind. I hate who we are—that someone could do this to another human being—to another shifter.

We're the monsters that humans write about.

Chapter 34

Arthur
THE HORNY TOAD

"Where is my mate?!"

I hear Nestor roar this behind me and feel a margin of relief that the bloke is ok. But I have my hands full with the pregnant woman who surely is about to give birth. It would make the most sense as to why the doctor had them all in the same room. Unfortunately, the odds are not looking great for the remaining three given the first two women's experience. Quite frankly, I'm terrified to see what they'll give birth to.

Our problems are compounded when, minutes later, the bizzies show up. They have us surrounded, and I know it doesn't look good. I see my dad and uncle looking around wildly for escape, but Nestor just appears deadly and ready to strike. His mate is missing, and he'll do anything to get her back—which makes him very dangerous. I think about what Belle said, and I take a deep breath knowing that what I'm about to do might be the last straw for my father and uncle.

"Listen, I'm Arthur—and I'm a Shifter," I announce to the cops. "Specifically I'm a horny toad—it's the type of animal I change into. All of us here, change into different animals. I know this sounds crazy, and I'll show you in a moment, but first, you have to know that we're only trying to help. Some of our kind have been hurting human women— human women like these ones right here. You can see two have already passed," I pause to point out the two dead women covered in blood and the three-headed dog shifter.

The group of sweenies[1] recoil in horror.

"I know it looks like some sick experiment—and to some extent, *it is*—but here in a little bit, this three-headed dog will turn into a baby just like the one that you see over there."

Everyone turns to stare at Gryffon, who just looks like an innocuous babe. Sian has managed to quiet him down again, and he appears deceivingly harmless.

"If we don't get these three women in medical care *now*, they will die just like the other two. They need to have C-sections. We... have no idea what kind of animals are inside them. I'm trusting you with our secret to do the right thing —another human once told me that we could trust you— should trust you. Please tell me that we haven't made the wrong choice."

With this, I shift into my horny toad. I scramble out of my clothes, and when the human fuzz spots me, more screaming ensues. I quickly shift back into my human form and stand there starkers.

"Now, you know... I realize it's a bit, er, strange, but please help us—their lives depend upon it."

"Do you all turn into that?" one of the bizzies stammers.

"No," Elise calls, "I'm a bird, and so is my girlfriend here."

"I'm an arse as is my cousin," Jack announces.

"We're all horny toads," Dageus says, pointing to himself, my da, and my uncle.

"I'm a cockchafer," Jude admits.

"And I'm a fish. Oh—and that's the Loch Ness Monster!" he adds, hitching a thumb towards Nestor.

"Don't ask him to shift!" I hastily command when one of the cops opens her mouth to ask. "As long as you know that we haven't kidnapped these women, we're square."

Jude steps forward to take over.

"Listen, I'm Doctor Webb. If we don't get these women to a medical facility, I can guarantee you they will die."

At this, the Chef Constable nods.

"I'll call the chopper," he announces and relief courses through me.

I'm glad that today we've gotten the Ravenglass area's finest, and they're taking the situation seriously. Only time will tell, though, the impact of humans knowing our secret.

"*Belle!*" Nestor moans by me, sobbing into his hands.

It's unnerving watching a man of such brute strength cry, but the truth is, we all feel his loss. Belle—she was part of us all, and now that piece is missing. I catch Nestor's eyes.

"We're going to get her back, I promise."

I don't make this vow lightly. After everything Belle has done for us, we *must* do the same for her. For now, we need to get the three remaining women to safety. My mind can barely process all the horrors they've been made to suffer because of the dean.

Injected with some concoction to go into heat.

Raped by my kind.

Forced to give birth to monstrous children—*to only then die.*

It makes me sick that the dean had so little care for

them. These women are nothing but a vessel to bring forth his creation—once they've served their purpose, they're disposable. Our time is limited to get back Belle, but we have something the dean and other Tershes will never expect—*human man power.*

I can only hope that the humans are *really* on our side.

Fifteen minutes later, the air ambulance lands, and we get the remaining three women loaded. Jude hesitates before declaring that he's going with them—somebody has to perform the surgery and explain.

"I'll go with him," my uncle offers.

"I will, too," my da volunteers, and I smile proudly at my kin.

The humans knowing goes against everything we've been taught, but my uncle and da are both willing to be ambassadors for our kind.

"I can go, too," Harry offers, but my uncle quickly refuses because, well, the crazy arse might not be the best representation.

"No," Jude agrees with my Laird. "You should go with Jack—*find Belle.*" He turns to Nestor, "Go get *our* mate."

The significance of his words is not lost on me. Jude is acknowledging Nestor's bond to Belle. As well as all of ours. *Our mate.* The words fill me with so much conflicting joy and despair—the only way to right my world is to get Belle back.

Jude gets into the helicopter; it quickly lifts up and flies away to the hospital. I send a quick prayer that the women will be ok. Somewhere in the insanity, the three-headed pup shifts into his human form. I hear Elise call him *'Cerberus'* and think it's absolutely fitting. The Chief Constable suggests that Elise, Sian, Gryff, and Cerebus be taken into custody for safety.

The humans might know our secret, but that doesn't mean we trust them explicitly. I know I'm the one who jumped into this situation with both feet, but desperate times call for desperate measures. This doesn't mean we can't still be smart and cautious. The birds and babies definitely need to be somewhere safer, though. Thankfully, Dageus and Harry have the foresight to go with them, leaving Theo, Jack, Nestor, and me to find our sweet Yank mate.

"Promise me you'll bring her back," Sian sobs as I hug her goodbye.

I kiss little Gryff on the forehead before turning to the dark-haired Cerberus and ruffle his silky head. He coos at me, and my heart melts to goop.

"I promise we'll bring her back," I finally answer Sian. "You take care of these little guys and Elise. We'll be back before you know it."

I watch the six of them leave and hope I didn't just lie to one of my best friends. Turning to Jack, I raise a brow.

"It's time to call your connections again," I murmur.

Quicker than lightning, he nods and pulls out his phone. My hands twitch in agitation. Every second that passes feels like hours. Who knows what the dean and his scientist are doing to Belle—I swiftly shut down these thoughts. I can't afford to play the what-if game right now. The guys need me to be focused—*Belle needs me to be focused.* Everything is at stake right now.

And time is running out.

Chapter 35

Belle

eing covered in dire wolf slobber is not nearly as sexy as it sounds.

In fact, now that I think about it, it's not sexy at all—it's downright disturbing and disgusting. Then again, it could be my own vomit and pee water. So, I suppose this time around I'm ahead of myself, right? I look around and find that I'm on a luxury yacht.

Of course, I am.

Where else would Dean Stiffdick be?

"Take her down to the clinic," he commands nonchalantly to Dr. Fuckface.

A doctor's clinic on a yacht?

Wow.

It takes hoity-toity *and* disturbing to a whole new level, but what do I expect with Dean Stiffdick?

"You mean the sick bay?" I sniff, trying to match his level of entitled superiority.

I must miss my mark because the assclown doesn't even

answer. Dr. Fuckface comes over to escort me *to the clinic*, and I kick him in the shins. In retrospect, it probably should have been the dick. When I try this, he shifts his leg up in protection.

"Don't push it!" he growls at me.

"No!" I snarl with anger, feeling a familiar tingle under my skin.

"It's *you* who shouldn't push *me!*"

As if I'd done it a thousand times, I easily and effortlessly shift into my chimera. Pride—and something a little more savage—courses through me. I open my mouth and roar ferociously.

My lion bares its sharp teeth.

My mamba hisses menacingly, ready to inject peeps with deadly venom.

My goat...well, it's just an idiot that I try to ignore.

At least two-thirds of me is terrifying, right?

But Dr. Fuckface doesn't look scared *at all*. I realize this is because he's still holding that damn syringe—which he plunges into my side and steps back quickly before I can swipe and gut him. As quickly as I shifted into my chimera, I collapse back into human form.

"What did you do?!" I manage to gasp through my panic.

I don't like lying there naked and vulnerable when I was just magnificent and deadly.

"For every action there's a reaction," Doctor Fuckface says simply.

"What the hell does that mean?!" I snap, regaining some of my anger.

Unfortunately, I don't feel the familiar burn of the shift.

"It means I turned you into an animal, and I just as easily unturned you out of it."

Fuck a duck.

My fears have been confirmed—I'm no longer a chimera.

I'm no longer strong.

And I wonder if I'm no longer anyone's mate.

Dean Hardwick comes sauntering up behind us.

"Take her down and get her hooked up so we can begin the procedure."

Without saying it, I know the dean means for me to be bred, but I escaped once. *Could I be lucky enough to do it twice?* If I were still my animal, there would be no question —they wouldn't be able to chain me down. My chimera was strong enough to pull apart the chains. It *was* the Highlander. Now, I'm just Belle again.

Stop it, you stupid whore, my brain snarks like a dillhole. *You escaped once using your own ingenuity—you can do it again!*

"Yeah!" I yell out loud.

Doctor Fuckface looks over at Dean Stiffdick.

"Who's she talking to?" the doc wonders.

"I don't know. This one's daft. Just take her away."

I give the dean a look.

He thinks I'm daft?

If this douchecanoe wants crazy, I'll show him crazy!

Psycho-bitch mode powers activated!

Dr. Fuckface pushes me through the ship and down the stairs, not having a clue about what's just happened inside my brain. Of course, this ship is more opulent than some apartments I've stayed in. It's mind boggling—*how does somebody have this much money to make basically a mansion on water?* I'm telling you right now that's not fair. One person should not have that much money when the rest of the world is suffering.

Do you know how many peanut butter and jelly sandwiches

I ate in undergraduate school because I didn't have enough money for a real meal and because I spent all my extra cash on male escorts?!

Well, when I defeat Dean Stiffdick, I plan on stealing his yacht as collateral.

We finally make it to the 'clinic, and Dr. Fuckface shoves me inside like the gentleman he's not. I feel another sharp sting in my arm, making me yelp.

"Would you quit that?!" I roar before collapsing.

I open my mouth to continue giving him a piece of my mind—but I can't.

I'm utterly and totally paralyzed.

The only thing that I can seem to move is my eyes. I roll them towards Dr. Fuckface in horror.

What did he do to me?

The evil scientist answers my unspoken question.

"I've injected you with chironex fleckeri. It's what the box jellyfish uses to paralyze their prey—before they eat them."

If I didn't know Doctor Fuckface's nefarious plan to use me to breed freak animals, I would be concerned he planned on eating me himself. The jerk of epic proportions scoops me up like I weigh nothing and tosses me onto a bed.

"No need to restrain you this time," he cheerfully points out. "Ahh, do you hear that? *Silence.* Someone should have paralyzed your mouth a long time ago."

This is only making me want to punch his teeth down his throat. Surprisingly, I think he'd look better without any teeth. The mad scientist starts hooking me up to various machines, and I mentally flinch when he inserts the IV. I feel the cool liquid starting to flow through my veins and pray it's just fluids... *the doc's smug smile suggests otherwise.*

The sound of multiple machines doing their work beeps around me as a monster disguised as a man hums and checks the readings.

Everything seems to be going ok until he does one test. Dr. Fuckface swiftly comes over and withdraws some blood. He shakes the vial up and just turns his back to me—what he does with it, I don't have a clue. What I *do* know is that when he turns back around, the familiar look of panic is on his face. You know, like before—when he injected me with something he shouldn't have.

I don't like this look.

It didn't bode well for me the last time, and I highly doubt it'll bode well for me *this* time.

Dr. Fuckface dashes out of the room, leaving me alone to worry about what's wrong now. It doesn't take long before he comes back with Dean Stiffdick. Both of them are talking loudly, not even bothering to disguise what's going on.

"We can't breed her!" the scientist is repeating over and over.

And he says *I* ramble.

"For fuck's sake—why the hell not?" Dean Stiffdick demands.

Yeah, I mentally shout, *why the hell not?*

"Because," the doctor sighs, handing Dean Stiffdick something. "She's *already* bred."

My mind blanks at these words, and it takes me a second to process his meaning, but when I do, the realization punches me in my paralyzed gut.

God damn those saints of broken condoms, I'm pregnant.

THE END FOR NOW

CLICK HERE to get your copy of KRAKEN UNDER PRESSURE (Shifters Anonymous Book 3)

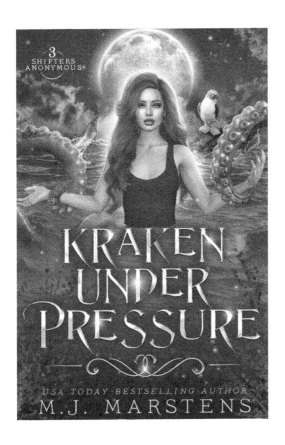

Hold on to your titties—it's coming!

(And by titties, I obviously mean the bird. Sheesh. Like I'm some kind of slippery dick trying to sneak in dirty things.)

CLICK HERE to get your copy of KRAKEN UNDER PRESSURE (Shifters Anonymous Book 3)

ENDNOTES

CHAPTER FIVE

1. The first floor in Britain is the second floor in the US.

CHAPTER SEX

1. Scottish for 'shut your mouth'

CHAPTER NINE

1. Scottish for 'to have a chat'

CHAPTER TWELVE

1. British for 'crazy person'

CHAPTER TWENTY

1. British word for 'crybaby'

CHAPTER THIRTY-FOUR

1. British word for 'cops'

ACKNOWLEDGMENTS

Thank you to: Beth Ann for all promo work you've done with this book; Annie, Heather, and Allison for beta reading, Jodie-Leigh for the amazing cover and pro tip about 'fanny flutters', A.J. for formatting (and being sexy), all my ARCers, and to you, my reader.

ABOUT MJ MARSTENS

Bestselling author M.J. Marstens mixes romance, suspense, comedy, and sassy characters who can say whatever they are thinking because it is just a story. When she is not creating steamy scenes or laugh-out-loud fiascos, she is refereeing her three children that she homeschools. In her free time, she loves to eat, sleep, and pray that her children do not turn out like the characters she writes about in her books.

Stay Connected

Join the Reader's Group for exclusive content, teasers and sneaks, giveaways, and more:
https://www.facebook.com/groups/MJMarstensNR

ALSO BY MJ MARSTENS

Liminal Academy Series:

Book 1: Evanescent

Book 2: Ephemeral

Book 3: Eternal

The Afflicted Zodiac Series:

Book 1: Virgo Rising

Book 2: Retrograde

Book 3: Total Lunar Eclipse

Assassins of the Shadow Society Series:

Book 1: Badass Alchemy

Fairy Tales Retold for RH:

Adventures in Sugarland

Imprismed: Captured in Rainbowland

Classics Retold for RH:

The Swan Empress

Legends Retold for RH:

Scaled

Once Upon a Time in December

An Irrevent RH Comedy:

Motherf*cker

A Dark Menage:

Unveiled

An RH Paranormal Comedy:

Mate Date

Hexed, Vexed, & Undersexed co-write standalone with A.J. Macey:

Hexed, Vexed, & Undersexed

Glitter & Ghosts co-write series with A.J. Macey:

Books 1-4: Titles TBA